"Everything, Pip," Jeremy murmured fervently, in a voice that was deep and pungent, yet sweet as honey. "And this is what I've been waiting for all night—the chance to take you in my arms and feel your soft curves embracing me."

He's only rehearsing, so don't go getting all stirred up, Pippi firmly ordered herself. It was good advice, but she completely ignored it nonetheless.

The glow in Jeremy's brown eyes was a kind of radiant energy that kissed her face with warmth as he gazed down at her. His left hand closed over her trembling knuckles, and the fingers of his right hand splayed across the small of her back like five fiery brands of possession. Pippi sighed as she brought her left hand up to rest on his broad shoulder. Slowly, savoring the moment, Jeremy drew her unresisting body close against his muscled chest and thighs.

They danced. Even amidst the crowd of moving, swaying couples, Pippi felt enfolded with Jeremy in a magic cloak of intimacy. Everywhere that his body touched hers through the thin silk of her dress, ripples of wildfire coursed over her skin. She was permeated by desire that ebbed and flowed in her like the pulsing beat of the music . . .

WHAT ARE *LOVESWEPT* ROMANCES?

They are stories of true romance and touching emotion. We believe those two very important ingredients are constants in our highly sensual and very believable stories in the *LOVESWEPT* line. Our goal is to give you, the reader, stories of consistently high quality that may sometimes make you laugh, sometimes make you cry, but are always fresh and creative and contain many delightful surprises within their pages.

Most romance fans read an enormous number of books. Those they truly love, they keep. Others may be traded with friends and soon forgotten. We hope that each *LOVESWEPT* romance will be a treasure—a "keeper." We will always try to publish

LOVE STORIES YOU'LL NEVER FORGET
BY AUTHORS YOU'LL ALWAYS REMEMBER

The Editors

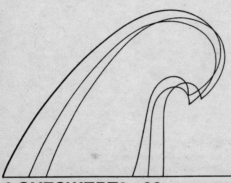

LOVESWEPT® • 93

Kathleen Downes
Practice Makes Perfect

 BANTAM BOOKS
TORONTO • NEW YORK • LONDON • SYDNEY • AUCKLAND

PRACTICE MAKES PERFECT
A Bantam Book / May 1985

*LOVESWEPT® and the wave device are registered
trademarks of Bantam Books, Inc. Registered in U.S. Patent
and Trademark Office and elsewhere.*

All rights reserved.
Copyright © 1985 by Kathleen Downes.
Cover artwork copyright © 1985 by Ken Joudry.
*This book may not be reproduced in whole or in part, by
mimeograph or any other means, without permission.*
For information address: Bantam Books, Inc.

ISBN 0-553-21697-X

Published simultaneously in the United States and Canada

---

*Bantam Books are published by Bantam Books, Inc. Its
trademark, consisting of the words "Bantam Books" and
the portrayal of a rooster, is Registered in U.S. Patent and
Trademark Office and in other countries. Marca Registrada.
Bantam Books, Inc., 666 Fifth Avenue, New York, New
York 10103.*

PRINTED IN THE UNITED STATES OF AMERICA

O   0 9 8 7 6 5 4 3 2 1

One

They lunged and sprang like armed gladiators in the bare, echoing, high-walled court. Every muscle of Jeremy's glistening torso seemed to flex with menacing power as his arm slashed forward in a deadly stroke that should have put his adversary right out of the contest.

But Pippi was in no mood to accept defeat tamely. Not today. Underneath the tangle of red curls that rioted above her white sweatband there was a matching tangle of emotions that demanded the physical release of hard, aggressive exercise.

She dove headfirst toward the ball, backhanding it with her racquet just in time before it took a second bounce. Her last-minute recovery caught Jeremy by surprise, and Pippi laughed as the hard rubber missile rocketed past his ankles. She had never come this close to beating him at racquetball before.

But "close" was as far as it went. When the game ended a few minutes later, Jeremy was the victor as usual. "Great game!" he panted as they left the court and headed for the showers. "I'll meet you out front in twenty minutes. Why don't we walk to the restaurant this morning, since it's so nice out?"

Pippi nodded in agreement and hurried into the women's locker room. As she stripped and showered, her body felt tingly and alive after the competitive workout, and the knot of raw anger inside her had eased a little. Now she could hardly wait for the full relief that would come once she'd told Jeremy the whole sordid story and then cried on his shoulder about what a creep Marc had turned out to be after all.

Of course, the first thing Jeremy would say was "I told you so," but Pippi didn't mind. He *had* told her so, and she should have listened. What was the good of having a wise, quiet, thoughtful friend like Jeremy Holt if you never took his advice? But you could always count on him to be patient and sympathetic after you landed in a mess, even when it was your own fault and could have been avoided if only you'd listened to him in the first place.

He was waiting for her outside in the spring sunshine, leaning against the side of the building with his hands stuffed into his pockets. A typical Jeremy pose. He greeted her with his usual shy grin, and for the umpteenth time Pippi found herself amazed at his transformation from the bold, lightning-quick opponent she faced on the racquetball court to the bashful, mild-mannered CPA who was the Jeremy Holt she knew and liked so well.

If she hadn't just seen him in action wearing nothing but a pair of gym shorts, Pippi would never have guessed at the sleek, superbly muscled strength that lay hidden beneath the neat brown crew neck sweater, blue Oxford-cloth shirt, and sedate tan slacks. She would never have believed that his warm brown eyes could gleam with ferocious fire, nor that his lean, rangy body could move with all the lethal grace and swiftness of an attacking lion.

Where did all that untamed animal energy disappear to when he put his clothes on? The question had occurred to Pippi more than once. But suddenly a new question teased at her thoughts—when Jeremy made love with a woman, which Jeremy would he be? Kind, tender, and unsure? Or as dangerous, unpredictable, and skillful at lovemaking as he was on a racquetball court? The thought was oddly disturbing.

Pippi quickly brushed aside the pictures conjured up by her too vivid imagination. There was no point in complicating their close, supportive friendship by indulging in silly fantasies. After all, Jeremy had made it plain he wasn't interested in her as a lover. That incident six months ago, just after her breakup with Rob, was admittedly rather fuzzy in her memory. Frankly, she'd had too much to drink that night. But she remembered one fact all too clearly. She'd practically thrown herself at Jeremy, and he'd rejected her.

Maybe that was why she'd been so quick to leap into her disastrous involvement with Marc. It had been a childish way of demonstrating that *somebody* wanted her. But the hurt hadn't gone away. That night was one of the few things she and Jeremy had never talked about. On the surface their friendship continued as before. Yet it made a difference, knowing there was one subject too painful and embarrassing ever to be mentioned between them.

But it wasn't worth thinking about. Actually,

Jeremy wasn't even her type. He probably made love as awkwardly as he made small talk at cocktail parties! And Pippi liked her men suave and confident and worldly. She sighed. Like Marc, the human reptile.

"You're awfully quiet today, Pip," Jeremy remarked as they strolled along, enjoying the warmth of the sunshine after the long Minnesota winter. "Anything wrong?"

"I'll tell you all about it over breakfast," Pippi promised, looking forward to his sympathy once she told him how badly Marc had behaved. She felt warmed by the genuine concern she heard in his voice and read in his dark brown eyes. "Right now I'm too hungry to talk."

"Okay. Actually . . ." Jeremy hesitated, and she was puzzled to see a faint flush mask his cheekbones. "Actually, I have something I want to discuss with you too."

"Well, it's only fair for me to listen to your troubles for a change," Pippi said encouragingly. "After all, I've been unloading my problems on you since the day we met. I just hope you won't be disappointed when you find out how bad I am at giving advice."

"Well, I didn't . . . That is, it's not . . ." But just then they arrived in front of the gaily striped awnings of the little restaurant where they often had breakfast after their Saturday racquetball matches, and Jeremy never did get around to finishing the sentence.

Pippi had never seen him so ill-at-ease before. They sat at their regular table near the window, but today Jeremy had trouble finding a suitable spot to put his long legs, and the waitress almost tripped over him when she came to take their order. He played nervously with the salt and pepper shakers on the pastel-colored tablecloth. His gaze kept accidentally encountering hers, and then darting over her head and out the window, up into the budding branches of the trees that lined the street.

Curiosity began to grow inside Pippi as she wondered what on earth Jeremy could have to tell her that had gotten him into such a state.

"Hey, relax!" she ordered him, laughing her usual husky laugh as she laid her hand soothingly on his. "We're *friends*, remember? Right now you remind me of the little boys I see in my studio—squirming in their tight collars, with their shiny dress-up shoes pinching their feet and their hair all plastered down against their heads. Sometimes it takes all my tricks and clown faces to convince them that having a picture taken isn't a method of torture! But *you* have no business being nervous with me, Jeremy. We've known each other too long for that."

"Sixteen months, two weeks, and three days," he said quietly.

"What?"

"That's how long we've known each other."

"Oh, you accountants are all alike—you've got to have exact numbers for everything!" she teased. "Are you sure you can't come up with a more precise figure than that? What about hours, minutes, and seconds?"

"Let me see. My appointment at your studio that day was for eleven, but I was ten minutes early, so that makes it—"

"Wait! I was only kidding!" she exclaimed, laughing. But his words had stirred up her own memories of their first meeting.

"I remember—that was the day I had triplets," she said blithely, much to the astonishment of the waitress who had come by to refill their coffee cups. "They were two-year-olds, and they looked adorable in their ruffled pink dresses and perky pink hair ribbons. But I could *not* get all three of them to sit still together long enough for me to get a good shot. One of them was always in motion. I was desperate."

"So you came rushing out into the waiting room, where I was calmly minding my own business, and practically dragged me into the studio to help you." Jeremy sounded as if he still found it hard to believe she'd commandeered his services that way. "Before I knew what hit me, I was doing Donald Duck imitations and generally making a fool of myself in front of three little girls, their mother, and you."

"You did *not* make a fool of yourself!" Pippi corrected him emphatically. "You did a great job. Even after all these months, I still get new customers who say they came to me because they loved that picture I did of the Jones triplets. And I couldn't have done it without your help."

Jeremy skeptically arched one brow. "That's funny. All this time I've had a sneaking suspicion that you could have coped with those triplets just fine on your own. I think you roped me into helping because you thought it would put me at ease for my own session in front of the camera."

Pippi gulped. How did he get to be so damn smart? "Uh—" she began.

"And as I recall, your strategy worked a little too well," he added with a smile.

"Not true! Those shots of you were marvelous!" she said. "How was I to know you'd have so many stuffy prejudices about what was 'appropriate' for a business portrait?"

"Face it, Pip. Even you should have been able to

figure out that an accountant has to project a certain image of trustworthiness and reliability. Prospective clients just would not have reacted favorably to a picture of me wearing a cheeky grin and a crooked tie."

"Hmph. Do you realize what a blow it was when you came back to the studio and informed me that *none* of the proofs I showed you was suitable?" she demanded.

"It would have been hard *not* to realize it, since you promptly burst into tears at the news."

"So unprofessional of me," Pippi said with a rueful shake of her head. "But I was already feeling like a total failure that day. After all, it was the first anniversay of my divorce."

"I remember," Jeremy said dryly. "You told me all about it."

She chuckled softly. "Poor Jeremy! I must have embarrassed you to death that day, weeping all over your three-piece suit. But you never complained. You just blushed bright red and handed me your handkerchief. And then you took me out for coffee and got me to tell you the story of my life."

"I'd never made a woman cry before," he confessed sheepishly. "I figured it was my responsibility to cheer you up again."

"Oh, yeah. You were great for my morale. You said my ex-husband sounded like a jackass, and that only a saint or a lunatic could have stayed married to a guy like that for three whole years."

"I just call 'em as I see 'em, sweetheart," he drawled in a voice that was vaguely reminiscent of Humphrey Bogart.

"Actually, you did make me feel lots better. Especially when you said you had a hunch that pretty soon I'd find somebody new and put the bad memories behind me. And you were right! Two days later I met Rob and fell for him. The only problem was—"

"That he was twice the jackass your ex-husband was," Jeremy interjected sourly. "Hardly what I had in mind when I suggested finding somebody new. But you refused to listen when I tried to point that out."

"Look on the bright side," Pippi said. "At least Rob and I never made the mistake of actually getting married. Though we must have broken our engagement and then patched it up again at least ten times," she added as an afterthought.

"At least. And *you* were always the one doing the patching. I've never seen anyone so determined to keep a pointless relationship going. Anyone else would have let it die quietly of natural causes after the first month." Jeremy sounded almost angry.

"Thank goodness I could count on your friendship through the whole ordeal," she said gratefully. "What would I do without you, Jeremy? Anytime I have trouble with the men in my life— and Lord knows, it seems to happen with amazing frequency—I can always count on you to help me over the rough spots."

"Oh, yes, there's always good old Jeremy to come to the rescue." His mobile, generous mouth tightened, and Pippi was puzzled by the bitter tone of his comment.

"I suppose you're a little fed up with me by now," she ventured hesitantly, feeling a sudden lump in her throat. But she tried to laugh. "After all, it must get pretty boring to hold my hand through one emotional crisis after another."

"Holding your hand is never boring, Pip," he said huskily. "But it's damn frustrating to see you making the same mistakes over and over again. You never learn."

"Falling in love isn't something you *learn*!" she burst out defensively. "It just *happens*!"

"But in your case it always 'happens' with some guy who's totally wrong for you. First your ex-husband, then Rob, and now Marc."

"I can't help it! Every time I fall in love, I'm always positive that *this* time it'll be different."

"But it never is," Jeremy responded stonily. "And how could it be, when the men you pick are always carbon copies of one another?"

"They are?"

"Haven't you noticed? They're cold, self-centered, irresponsible jerks. They like to throw their weight around, and they love to impress people with that shallow pseudo-charm of theirs. Pip, they feed off your warmth and vitality and generosity without giving anything in return, and you let them! Then, when it's over, you come crying to *me*. Don't I have a right to be fed up?"

Pippi's face was paper-white with shock, and her mouth began to tremble. Jeremy had never lashed out at her like this before. Never. And his criticism of her taste in men had never been so blisteringly harsh. He had no right to say such things! Not even if they were close to the truth.

"Oh, hell, I've made you cry again," he muttered, and Pippi felt an odd rush of relief as she saw the familiar look of caring return to Jeremy's brown eyes.

Until that moment she hadn't realized how much she depended on him. His friendship had become a solid anchor in the stormy ups and downs of her failed relationships. She hated to think how she'd feel if he decided she was a hopeless case and washed his hands of her.

"I'm sorry, Pip." He fumbled in his pocket for the pristine white monogrammed handkerchief he always carried. "I didn't mean to hurt you. It's just . . ."

"I understand," she said, giving him a watery smile as she dabbed at the tears on her cheeks. "I've been thoughtlessly taking advantage of your patience and kindness and politeness, and you should have said something sooner! If only I'd known you felt this way, I would have stopped pestering you with my silly problems a long time ago."

He groaned. "That's not what I meant at all, Pip! I *like* it when you confide in me. But . . ."

Just then the waitress finally appeared with their order, and both Jeremy and Pippi were silent while plates of omelets, fresh fruit, and whole wheat toast were set down before them.

Pippi didn't think she could manage to eat a single bite. Her hunger seemed to have evaporated right along with her plans for telling Jeremy about her breakup with Marc. No way could she confess to him that yet another relationship had ended in failure, not after the conversation they'd just had. She was through burdening poor Jeremy with the details of her luckless love life. From now on she'd just have to muddle through on her own.

"So, didn't you say there was some problem you were going to tell me all about over breakfast?" Jeremy asked. The butter knife slipped from Pippi's fingers and clattered loudly against her plate. Her head was bent and her cheeks were pink as she retrieved the knife and carefully set about scraping the squashed pat of butter off the table-cloth.

"Oh, no big deal," she said miserably. She hated lying. "One of those impossible-to-please customers got me upset at work yesterday, that's all. I'd rather just forget it. Really. But what about you?" she asked brightly, eager to change the subject.

"You mentioned earlier there was something *you* wanted to discuss."

His face seemed to close up as if he were a panic-stricken turtle retreating into his shell. "Oh. That," he said weakly. Pippi was shocked to see how his hand trembled as he set down his coffee cup.

"Jeremy, what's wrong?" she asked softly. "Would you rather wait and talk about it some other time?"

"No. I've put it off too long already. I'll go crazy if I have to keep trying to hide the way I feel."

"Then tell me." Her voice was firm and gentle, and she reached out to stroke his whitened knuckles where his hands gripped the edge of the table. "Whatever it is, I promise I'll do my best to help."

He gave a choked, painful laugh. "Oh, Pip, you're too much! Can't you see I'm trying to tell you . . ." His voice seemed to fail him.

"What?" she prompted, confused.

His answer, when it came, was spoken so softly and his head was bent so low that Pippi couldn't catch all the words.

"You're in love?" she asked uncertainly, not sure if that was what he'd been trying to say or not.

He nodded mutely, and she experienced a sudden pang of dismay. The idea of Jeremy in love with someone was oddly painful. But she should have expected it sooner or later. Just because he'd never shown any signs of regarding *her* in a romantic or sexual way didn't mean he was immune to those feelings where the right woman was concerned. Ever since that humiliating night six months earlier, she had known better than to wish for more than friendship from Jeremy. And now even their friendship might fall by the wayside once he became involved with another woman.

But these were selfish, unworthy thoughts. A true friend would be thinking of Jeremy's happiness right now, not feeling sorry for herself. So Pippi forced a smile to her lips and glanced across the table at Jeremy. A straight, silky swathe of his light-brown hair had fallen forward over his eyes, and she instinctively brushed it back.

His head rose warily at her touch and his muscles tensed as if he were bracing himself for a blow. It was obvious that he cared about her reaction to his announcement, and the defiant vulnerability in his gaze clutched at her heart. This man was her friend, and he could so easily be hurt.

A wave of protectiveness swelled up inside her, and she felt a surge of anger against this unknown woman who had such power to wound Jeremy. But that was silly. Why should she assume this other woman would end up hurting him? Only a fool could fail to appreciate Jeremy's many lovable qualities, and surely he wouldn't have fallen in love with a fool.

"Who is she?" Pippi asked. "Do I know her?"

Jeremy blinked, and a tremor of strong emotion passed over his face. Twice he opened his mouth to speak, but no sound came out.

A sudden earth-shattering thought occurred to her. "Omigosh! Jeremy! It *is* a *woman* you're talking about, isn't it? You're not trying to tell me you're . . ."

He uttered a hoarse, strangled sound that could have been either a laugh or a moan. "I've gotta hand it to you, Pip—you sure know how to build up a man's ego!" he growled. "But let me reassure you. *Yes*, she's a woman, and *no*, I'm not gay!"

His aggrieved glare made Pippi want to slide right under the table. "Oops! Forgive me, Jeremy. It's just that you seemed so nervous about what you were telling me, and all at once it just popped into my head that *that* might be why. But if I'd stopped to think before I opened my big mouth—"

"And when was the last time you did *that?*" he interjected knowingly.

"—then I'd have realized that the whole idea just didn't fit somehow," she finished. "It's not *you.*"

"You better believe it's not *me!*" he muttered.

Fearing another explosion of his righteous indignation, Pippi tried a hasty change of subject. "This woman you're in love with. Does she know how you feel?"

"About what?"

"About *her.* That you love her, I mean."

"She doesn't have a clue."

"Oh." Pippi's forehead puckered with worry. "May I ask how she feels about you?"

He sighed, and a bitter smile twisted his lips. "Let's just say she thinks of me as a friend."

"Well, that's not a bad start. Friendship can blossom into love. But, it's a tricky process. You have to be careful to nurture it along just right." She took a deep breath. "And that's why you need *me* to help you."

"What?"

"You needn't look so shocked. "I *am* rather an expert when it comes to falling in love, you know. And it sounds like you could use a little expert advice right now. I'd be happy to give you a few pointers."

She waited anxiously for his reply, trying to decipher the peculiar expressions that flitted across his face. She was determined to help him, if only he'd let her! Obviously he didn't have the faintest idea how to go about courting this mysterious woman-friend of his, and if he weren't careful, he'd wind up with his heart all smashed to pieces. Pippi couldn't bear the thought.

"What do you say?" she prodded. "Isn't it about time I started paying you back for all the help you've given me?"

"I don't believe this!" Jeremy groaned and dropped his forehead against his clenched fists. "Forget it, Pip. The whole thing's impossible!"

"But why?" She looked at him for a moment in puzzled silence, and then her lips tightened. "Oh, I get it. You think just because my own love life is such a shambles, I've got no business telling you how to run yours."

"No, Pip, it's nothing like—"

"I don't blame you for feeling that way," she said quickly. "It's true that I've made mistakes. But that doesn't mean I can't see clearly when someone else's heart is involved instead of my own. And whether you like it or not, I'm going to give you one piece of very good advice." She paused and then spoke with dramatic emphasis. "Whatever you do, *don't* just announce to this woman, right out of the blue, that you've fallen in love with her. *That* would be fatal."

Jeremy's head shot upright and his brown eyes held a mixture of shock and confusion. Slowly they narrowed to mere slits of probing light. When he spoke, there was an odd intensity in his voice. "Perhaps you'd better explain that, Pip."

"If she thinks of you as just a friend, how's she going to feel if you suddenly tell her point-blank that you love her? I can tell you the answer right now—embarrassed, confused, and *unprepared!* Because *you* haven't taken the time and trouble to make her fall in love with you!"

"But . . . how would I do that? And besides, I don't want to *make* her do anything! Shouldn't it just happen naturally if it happens at all?" he protested wistfully.

She gave a gentle sigh. "Tell me, Jeremy, what would happen to a gardener who didn't bother to prepare the soil, but just threw seeds out on the hard ground and left them there without even watering them?"

"He wouldn't get much of a crop. But—"

"But wouldn't that method be more 'natural?' "

"I see your point, Pip, but love is hardly the same as gardening! How the hell am I supposed to *prepare* someone to fall in love with me? Dump a load of fertilizer on her?"

She couldn't help but look amused. "It's called seduction, Jeremy. And people have been doing it for years. Why don't you give it a try?"

He stared at her for several seconds. At first there was no way of guessing what thoughts were passing through his mind. Then Pippi saw the excitement begin to glimmer in his eyes, and she felt like cheering.

"Okay," he said breathlessly. "I'll try it. It's absolutely crazy, but I'll try it!" He flashed her a dazed, incredulous, reckless grin. "What do I do first?"

"First, you put ideas into her head! You make her aware of you as a man, not just a friend. You start her wondering what you're like in bed. But of course you've got to be careful not to come on too strong," Pippi added quickly. "Subtlety is the key. You don't want her to guess what you're up to just yet."

His shoulders slumped. "But how do I *do* all that? I wouldn't even know where to begin."

"It's easy, Jeremy! A little eye contact, a casual touch on the shoulder, an elusive trace of suggestiveness in your voice, and an enigmatic smile. That's all it takes. And then you might try a compliment, something like 'How come I never noticed what long, gorgeous eyelashes you have?' And then—"

"I can't do it, Pip."

He sounded so grimly positive that Pippi held back the superficial words of encouragement that were quivering on the tip of her tongue. "It's just not your style, is it?" she admitted. "Of course I could *teach* you, but . . ."

"Teach me?" he repeated thoughtfully. "You mean with role-playing and practice sessions and all that?"

"Sure, if that's what you'd like," she said, pleased to see his renewed enthusiasm. "When do you want to start?"

"Is tonight too soon?"

Pippi burst out laughing. "You can't wait to get this over with, can you?" she teased. "I promise it'll be painless. By the time I'm through with you, you'll be sweeping women off their feet by the hundreds!"

"I'll settle for just the one," he said softly.

"Fair enough. Lessons start tonight at my place. I'll make a batch of popcorn and then we can get to work."

"Popcorn?"

"It stimulates the brain cells. And we've got lots of high-powered thinking and planning to do. You see, we won't just be practicing our fleeting sensuous glances. We've got to work out the long-term strategy for your entire courtship!"

"I thought it was a seduction."

"Seduction, courtship, it all boils down to the same thing in the end. And we need to come up with a few battle plans!"

"Hey, General Patton, *sir*, we're talking about

love here, not war," Jeremy pointed out in a voice of amused protest.

"You think I'm getting carried away?"

"Just a tad, Pip."

"Maybe you're right. It's just that I'm practically bursting with ideas for how you can get this woman to sit up and take notice of you, Jeremy! The most important thing at this stage is to get her attention on a physical level." She paused. "Tell me, Jeremy—have you ever kissed her?"

"Uh . . . well . . . Actually, no, but she's kissed *me*. Sort of. Just in passing. Does that count?" Pippi shook her head. "I didn't think so. Are you trying to tell me I should? Right away?" She nodded. "But wouldn't that be rather . . . obvious?"

"Not if you handle it right. You've got to make it brief and casual and friendly. A spur-of-the-moment kind of thing. She mustn't guess that you've planned it."

"Sounds like a piece of cake," he said gloomily.

"You'll manage." She gave him a cheerful smile, then glanced at her watch. "Omigosh! I've got to run! I should have been at the studio half an hour ago." She made a hasty estimate of her share of the breakfast tab, shoved some money on the table, and stood up. "See you tonight."

"Wait." He took her hand just as she was turning to go. "I want you to know how much this means to me, Pip." His upturned face conveyed such a poignant depth of emotion that Pippi felt stirred almost to tears. Her hand trembled in the warm clasp of his fingers. "I'm grateful for your help," he said huskily. "Very grateful."

And then it happened. Before Pippi could quite read the intent in his warm, glowing eyes, he reached up and drew her face down to his. All the noises of the crowded restaurant—the buzz of strangers' conversations and the rattling of plates and silverware—seemed to dim and grow silent as his lips brushed hers.

A swift, bright shaft of sweet sensation traversed her consciousness and then was gone, all in the space of a mere heartbeat. The kiss was over as soon as it had begun, and the normal sounds of the world returned to Pippi's ears. Everything was going on as before. No one had even noticed. Only she was left shaken and confused.

Jeremy smiled up at her. "Well, how'd I do?" he asked nervously.

"Huh?" Her mind was a gaping void.

"Wasn't that the kind of kiss you meant? Should I be doing something differently? I want to get it right before I actually try it on *her*, you know."

"Oh. *Her.* Oh, of course. You were just *practicing.*" Pippi laughed, a bit breathlessly. "Well, you've got nothing to worry about! That was perfect. You'll have her eating out of your hand in no time flat."

"Thanks, Teach. And I really do appreciate what you're doing."

"My pleasure," she croaked, hurriedly tugging her hand free of his and backing away. She wasn't ready for another impromptu "rehearsal" just now! "I've really got to go."

"See you tonight, then."

Tonight. As she hurried out of the restaurant, Pippi found herself speaking aloud the thought that was drumming in her brain. "Oh, Lord. *What have I done?*"

Two

The fragrance of hot buttered popcorn greeted Jeremy as he climbed the last flight of stairs to Pippi's attic apartment. Before he even had a chance to knock, the door was flung open and Pippi's husky, irrepressible laughter welcomed him.

"Jeremy! What on earth possessed you to bring all these flowers?" she exclaimed. Her periwinkle blue eyes lit up with surprised pleasure as he placed the huge bouquet of creamy, mauve-tipped carnations in her hands.

"I figured they'd help get us in the mood for our practice session tonight," he said. "And here's a bottle of wine. I don't know how well it'll go with popcorn, but . . ."

"My, my. Wine and flowers. Maybe you don't need me to teach you anything about courting a woman after all!" she said with a teasing smile. "The flowers are beautiful." Bending her head, she took a deep breath of their fresh, enchanting scent. Jeremy watched as her glowing red curls tumbled forward, exposing the creamy white nape of her slender neck.

"I'm glad you like them," he mumbled, concentrating on removing his jacket and hanging it on the old-fashioned wooden coatrack that stood near the door.

"I *love* them," she assured him. "Now, you go ahead and sit down while I put these in water and open that bottle of wine."

Jeremy lowered his tall frame into the comfortable burgundy-colored sofa by the freestanding fireplace. The heat of the crackling fire felt good after the damp chill outside, and as he gazed around the room he felt once again the vivid, eclectic warmth of Pippi's apartment flowing into him like the glow of a fine red wine.

Tucked up under the eaves of a gaunt, faded, old three-story house, the large attic room was like the cozy nest of a magpie with charming but undisciplined taste. Wicker chairs, brass lamps, an antique armoire, crowded bookshelves made of bricks and boards, a braided rug, plump cushions in bright fabrics, and a profusion of ferns and other greenery all expressed the colorful exuberance of Pippi's personality.

The walls and the sloped attic ceilings were populated by a diverse array of human faces captured for an instant, forever, by Pippi's camera lens. Along with the photographs, she had unconsciously displayed her love for her work, her fascination with people, her compassion for their tragedies, and her sense of humor at their quirks and absurdities. So much of her private self was revealed there that Jeremy felt faintly ashamed of his own avid interest. It was almost like snooping through the pages of someone's diary.

A small shriek suddenly sounded from the other side of the bamboo partition that divided the main room from the tiny kitchen area. It was followed by a series of reverberating clangs and clatterings, as if some heavy metal object was in the process of falling a considerable distance.

"Pip, are you all right?" Jeremy shouted, crossing the room in three headlong strides.

"Um . . . not exactly," she answered in a quavering voice. His heart stopped beating for an instant when he saw her, clinging to the very top of the cupboards over the counter, her makeshift stepladder of cookbooks and cutting board toppling sideways on the counter beneath her dangling feet.

In a split-second he was there. His hands clamped around her hips and he lifted her down and back against his chest. They stood motionless while he tried to calm the adrenaline that was still pumping madly through his veins, speeding his pulse and his breathing. A warm blur of sensation informed him how soft and fragile Pippi's body felt in his hands. Was he really trembling, or was that her?

"What the hell were you trying to do?" he panted, squeezing her hard against him before letting her go.

"I was trying to get *that* down to put the flowers in." She pointed up at the heavy old pickling crock decoratively perched on top of the cupboard, side by side with a Chinese bamboo steamer and an arrangement of dried cattails. "But that darn copper fondue pot was in the way, and when it fell I made a grab for it and lost my balance, and *then* the cookbooks slid out from under my feet—"

"Stop!" Jeremy ordered. "You're giving me nightmares! Promise me, Pip, that you'll never try anything like this again. Of all the foolish, asinine ways to put yourself in the hospital, this really—"

"You just don't understand what it's like to be short," she retorted. "It's easy for you to lecture me, but when was the last time you couldn't just reach right up and grab whatever you wanted? Short people have to be creative."

"But all you had to do was ask and I would've gotten that darn thing down for you! Instead, you try to break your neck!"

"All right, I admit I made a mistake. But I hate asking other people to do things for me. I'm an adult. I should be able to get a pickling crock down from my own cupboard without calling in a man to do it for me!" She sighed deeply. "But since you're here, would you mind . . . ?"

"No problem." He smiled and swung himself lightly up onto the counter. He handed the heavy earthenware crock carefully to Pippi, and then climbed down again.

"It's so unfair," she muttered, watching his long legs flex as he landed on the floor like a gymnast completing his routine. "But thanks anyway."

He picked up the tray on which she had set the wine bottle, two glasses, and a bowl of popcorn. "I'll carry this."

"Thank you. I'll bring the flowers out in just a minute."

As soon as Jeremy left the kitchen, Pippi slumped against the counter. She didn't think she'd given herself away. Anyone would have screamed under those circumstances. But it was stupid to be so afraid of heights that she panicked merely from getting up on the kitchen counter! Forcing herself to go through with it hadn't been such a great idea, however. Thank goodness

Jeremy had been there. And at least he hadn't guessed how terrified she was.

She couldn't believe she was still shaking. That was just silly. Especially since it wasn't even the memory of her fear that was making her feel so weak. This latest tremor within her had more to do with the way Jeremy's arms had felt as he pressed her against him. But she refused to think about that.

Abruptly, she picked up the armload of carnations resting against the edge of the sink, thrust them helter-skelter into the earthenware crock, and filled the improvised vase with water.

"Let's get this show on the road," she said briskly as she carried the flowers into the living room. "We've got a lot of work to do."

"We sure do," Jeremy acknowledged glumly. "Where do you suggest we begin?"

"At the beginning, of course. First of all, how do you plan to greet your friend next time you see her? And that reminds me—what *is* her name? I can't go on calling her 'your friend' or 'this woman' all the time."

"Um . . . Mary. Her name is Mary."

Pippi sighed enviously. Though she didn't have a particularly envious nature, she'd spent her whole life envying people with nice normal names like Mary. Or John or Susan or Robert. People who could breeze through life's introductions and first encounters unencumbered by a name that provoked cute remarks, startled glances, and outright snickering.

Her mother had meant well. After all, it was only natural for a children's librarian to have a certain fondness for the childhood classics. But when it came to naming your daughters after your favorite characters, surely that was carrying things too far! Pippi and her sisters certainly thought so.

It wasn't so bad for Charlotte, the eldest, because not many people knew she was named after a talking spider. But Arrietty, the middle sister, had never quite forgiven her mother for naming her after one of the little people in *The Borrowers*. And Pippi had spent her childhood secretly trying to live up to her namesake—the intrepidly adventurous redhead, Pippi Longstocking.

"Earth to Pippi—come in, Pippi!" Jeremy interrupted her thoughts.

"Huh?"

"Before you get completely lost in outer space, may I remind you that I'm still waiting with bated breath to hear what I should say to . . . Mary, next time I see her."

"Oh, right! Sorry, Jeremy." Pippi laughed apologetically. "I was just thinking how simple life must be for people named Mary."

"Not necessarily," he demurred in a suspiciously innocent voice. "Just imagine if a *man* were named Mary. His life would be anything but simple."

She glared at him. "Do all accountants share your annoying habit of taking everything so literally?"

"No, not *all* accountants," he answered, poker-faced. "Only approximately ninety-three point nine percent of us—"

She groaned and flung a handful of popcorn at him. Jeremy gave her an unrepentant grin and began to eat the fluffy kernels that had scattered across his chest and into his lap.

"Mmm, good," he said, licking a trace of butter-flavored salt off his lips. "But you still haven't told me what I'm supposed to say to Mary."

"It's not *what* you say that's important at this point—it's *how* you say it. Show me what you can do with a basic 'Hello, Mary.' "

Jeremy cleared his throat. "Hello, Mary," he repeated awkwardly.

"That was fine. Now try it again, and this time put a little more feeling into it. Remember, you want the sound of your voice to turn her bones to firewater."

"I do?"

"Yes, you do. Now let's hear it."

"Hel*lo*, Mary," he drawled lasciviously.

"Omigosh!" Pippi giggled. "You sound like Count Dracula with a head cold."

The look of outrage on Jeremy's face silenced her laughter. "What do you want from me?" he demanded. "If this is your idea of help, then I'd just as soon forget the whole damn thing!"

"Sorry. I wasn't being very constructive in my criticism, was I? Let's try again. But this time don't put so much innuendo into it. You don't want to *leer* at her, you just want a certain lingering caressive quality in your voice. You want to leave her wondering why her pulse starts humming every time you speak."

Jeremy sighed. "Maybe you'd better show me how it's done."

"Good idea." She concentrated for a second, and then spoke, threading her voice with just a gossamer touch of sensuality: "Hello, Jeremy."

He fell back against the sofa cushions and stared at her. "Wow! I see what you mean. But there's no way I could ever say it like *that.*"

Pippi found herself blushing. "Nonsense. All it takes is practice." She wasn't about to admit that a certain something in her voice just now had caught even *her* by surprise.

His lips tightened. "How convenient. No need to bother with genuine emotion. Forget spontaneity and romance. All it takes is practice."

She stared at him in dismay. Why was he so touchy tonight? "It's not as cold-blooded as you make it sound," she said.

"Oh, really?" he asked sarcastically.

"Yes, really! It's like playing the piano. You have to learn to hit all the right notes before you can start to put the meaning and the passion into the music. So what's so terrible about running through a few scales before you go on stage for your virtuoso performance with Mary?"

"Nothing, I guess," he admitted. He certainly didn't look too happy about it. "Okay, I'll *practice!* I'll practice till the cows come home if that's what it takes! But I refuse to practice on someone who isn't even here. Forget this 'Hello, Mary' business. From now on it's 'Hello, Pippi.' "

"Oh, but . . . what if you got confused and accidentally said 'Hello, Pippi' to *Mary?"*

"I hardly think that's likely," he said in a coolly amused tone that made Pippi feel less than two inches tall. What had she been thinking of? Of course Jeremy would never get her confused with Mary, the woman he loved.

"Hello, Pippi." He tried the words out on his tongue very softly, and Pippi felt a shiver run down her spine. Jeremy was obviously a fast learner.

He deepened his voice so it was tinged with a faint huskiness, and repeated the words. "Hello, Pippi."

She drew a shaky breath. "Um . . . that's very good. You seem to be getting the hang of—"

"Hello, Pippi." Her faltering comment was cut off by the rich, deep tones of his voice, flowing dark and sweet as melted chocolate, yet laced with the rough, fiery taste of whiskey.

She tore her gaze away from his face and gulped down the rest of the wine in her glass. "Omigosh," she said softly, staring into the hot, glowing embers of the fire. "I think I've created a monster."

Jeremy gave a pleased laugh. "Was I that good?" His voice was back to normal now.

"You know you were. No woman will ever be safe with you again."

"Thanks . . . I think. So what's the next step, now that I've learned to say hello?"

"You've learned a lot more than that!" Pippi hastened to inform him. "Don't you see? Now you can use that same subtly suggestive tone of voice to add special significance to *anything* you say."

"Even if I'm talking about the weather?"

"Even if you're talking about soybean futures on the commodities market! But I wouldn't overuse it if I were you," she cautioned. "Save it for the occasions when it'll have the most impact."

"Such as?"

"When you make a conventionally polite remark that *could* have deeper feelings behind it. For instance, the phrase 'It's good to see you again' might mean exactly nothing. Or it might have enough traces of hidden meaning in it to make Mary swoon at your feet."

"It's good to see you again, Pip," he murmured experimentally. The velvet was back in his voice, yet it seemed to cut like a sharp-edged blade. Pippi didn't swoon, but she was grateful for the solid support of the couch beneath her.

"Obviously you don't need any more rehearsals." She managed a smile, though it felt rather flimsy on her lips.

"What's next then? This morning you mentioned something about eye contact," he suggested helpfully.

"Did I?" She swallowed. "I sure was full of bright ideas this morning, wasn't I?"

"Yes, you were very encouraging," Jeremy said, responding to the surface meaning of her words rather than the ironic tone with which she had uttered them. "You gave me hope, Pip."

Damn. She couldn't let him down now. He was obviously counting on her for help. And she *had* volunteered for this job, after all. No one had forced it on her. It was silly to let all this practicing make her uncomfortable, since it was only make-believe.

"So, you want to know about eye contact?" she said brightly. He nodded. And his intent gaze never left her face as she began to explain how he could make effective use of this very important technique in the art of seduction.

A half hour later Pippi was feeling quite dizzy. Or at least that's how she chose to describe the peculiar sensation that grew more overpowering each time Jeremy turned the full force of his warm, ardent brown eyes on her.

But it wasn't just his eyes. He had also remembered her advice on the effectiveness of an enigmatic smile. After a few tries, his smiles were very enigmatic. And *very* effective.

Then he felt the need to perfect the "casual touch on the shoulder" technique that she'd also mentioned that morning. But he was such a quick and resourceful pupil that he soon mastered the casual touch on the hand as well.

Over time the cumulative effect was quite disturbing to Pippi's equilibrium. But that was nothing compared to what happened when Jeremy decided to try all his new tricks at once in a coordinated effort.

He took her hand, and his eyes probed hers with a searching, sensual flame. His mouth curved in an elusive half-smile that vanished before Pippi could decipher its meaning. And then he spoke in that voice that suggested everything and promised nothing.

"I'll never forget tonight, Pip. You've taught me so much." He made it sound as if she'd just shared with him the deepest secrets of the universe and of life itself. Secrets so solemn and intimate and sublime that he and she were now inextricably bound together by their shared knowledge.

Pippi gave her head a bemused shake. The heat of the fire suddenly felt too intense on her skin and the heady scent of the carnations filled her nostrils like a narcotic vapor. A tingling warmth traveled up her arm from the gentle pressure of Jeremy's hand.

His face, so close to hers, seemed altered by some trick of the firelight. The hard angles of his jaw and cheekbones were thrown into relief, and unexpected threads of glinting gold were revealed in his hair. His eyes were so dark and intense, they were like the eyes of a stranger.

It occurred to Pippi that she was, quite literally, seeing Jeremy in a new light. And it made her very nervous. Her task was to help him woo another woman. She had no business getting all fluttery inside while he rehearsed with her the scenes he would play for real with Mary!

"It's time for me to get out my yellow notepads and sharpen some number two pencils," she announced abruptly.

He blinked. "What?"

"For our planning session. Remember? So far

we've just been working on the basics—the building blocks of a competent seduction. Now we've got to come up with plans for putting them all together."

"Oh." He looked doubtful. "Pip, I'm not sure I'm ready. Don't you think we should have a few more nights of practice?"

She gave a hollow laugh. "Definitely not. You underestimate yourself, Jeremy. Trust me—you've done a brilliant job so far. Now it's time to move on to the next step."

He didn't look convinced, but Pippi got up to bring out two legal-size pads of yellow paper and a fistful of freshly sharpened pencils. She arranged them neatly on opposite sides of the round oak dining table near the kitchen, and seated herself on one of the ladderback wooden chairs.

"What's wrong with the couch?" Jeremy asked.

"I can think better here," she replied airily. No way was she going to venture back to the cozy intimacy of that couch with Jeremy!

He sighed and looked decidedly unenthusiastic as he moved to the table. Then, instead of sitting across from her as she had intended, he pulled up a chair and sat down right at her elbow. She was terribly conscious of his nearness as she doodled nervously on the lined yellow paper.

"You don't seem to have come up with any earth-shattering ideas so far," he said, gesturing toward the intricate spiral pattern that was the only thing she'd produced on her businesslike pad of paper.

"Doodling helps me concentrate," she informed him haughtily. "And would you mind not breathing down my neck? It's distracting." And how! The skin at the nape of her neck was quivering as if caressed by a feather.

"Sorry." He moved away awkwardly and Pippi

sneaked a swift, guilty glance at him. His head was bent so she couldn't see his face, but his ears were red.

"No, *I'm* sorry," she said, putting her hand on his arm. "I shouldn't have snapped at you. Come on, let's put our heads together and come up with a strategy that'll make Mary fall right into your arms."

She might not have phrased it in quite that way if she'd remembered Jeremy's tendency to take things literally. When she'd said, "Let's put our heads together," she certainly hadn't envisioned that she and Jeremy would end up practically cheek to cheek as they worked on their list of ideas.

Pippi did her best to concentrate on the task at hand despite the prickle of awareness she felt each time she caught a whiff of the sandalwood soap Jeremy must have showered with earlier that evening. His clean-shaven jaw was smooth and hard, she noted. His eyelashes were long and thick. . . .

Impatient, she jerked her thoughts away from the path down which they were wandering. She centered her attention firmly on the yellow rectangle in front of her and finally, after several minutes of chewing on her pencil and drawing more doodles, she jotted down a few possibilities.

"That's my contribution," she announced.

"I can't think of anything," Jeremy confessed apologetically.

"Then I'd better not hear any complaints from you about these suggestions," she warned him with mock severity.

"Yes, *ma'am*. It looks to me like a very good list. Except for item number one."

"Now, just a minute! That's my best idea!"

"But—"

"What could be more romantic and sensually

titillating than an evening of dancing? Picture yourself with Mary in your arms, her hair brushing your cheek, her body pressed against yours, and both of you moving to a single, sensuous rhythm!"

"Yes, but—"

"And the beauty of it is, two people can dance together even if they're just casual acquaintances. The act of dancing doesn't presume intimacy or even attraction. So it's a quick way to make Mary aware of you in the physical sense, without being crude or obvious."

"Pip, I'm sure everything you say is true. There's just one problem. I don't know how to dance."

"Oh." She felt like a punctured balloon, but she managed a feeble grin. "So much for that idea."

"Aren't you giving up too soon? There must be a way of salvaging such a brilliant strategy."

"I don't see how," she replied mournfully. "You can't very well go dancing with someone if you can't dance."

"True. But that doesn't mean I can't *learn*." He paused, and Pippi saw that his ears were turning red again. "Couldn't you teach me?" he suggested hesitantly.

She should have seen it coming, but his request hit her like the slap of a breaking wave against her face. She felt a panicky, choking sensation, as if she'd just swallowed half an ocean, as if a dangerous undertow were tugging at her, threatening to carry her out to sea.

"No," she said instantly. "It would never work."

"Sure it would," he said, coaxing her. "You're a marvelous teacher, and I'll bet you're a marvelous dancer too. Just think how successful our lessons were tonight! Why should learning to dance be any different?"

She couldn't tell him that was exactly what she

was afraid of—that it *wouldn't* be any different at all. That it would be just as unnerving as tonight had been. That she'd find his nearness affecting her in the same startling, unwelcome way.

"Please, Pip," he murmured, laying his hand over hers where it rested on the table. "It means so much to me."

His pleading eyes seemed to pluck the answer from her very throat. "Okay." She sighed. "If you insist."

"Thank you." His smile could have melted marble and his voice rippled silkenly in her ears. His *voice.* Pippi stiffened. Too late, she realized exactly what voice he was using!

"So I've been had." She kept her tone coolly amused. "Isn't it just a bit unchivalrous to take the tricks *I* taught you and turn them into weapons against me?"

"All's fair in love and war," he said cheerfully.

"I hope you're joking, because that's a sentiment I strongly disagree with. Any love that's won with tricks and lies, without mutual respect and fair play, is hardly likely to bring lasting satisfaction to anyone."

He looked startled. Guilt and chagrin were written all over his face. But then his eyes narrowed in sudden speculation. "If you really feel that way, what's the point of all these 'tricks' you've been teaching me?" he challenged.

"That's different. Those are just techniques to attract Mary's attention, to make her take a fresh look at you. You want her to see you as you really are—a strong, caring, compelling man who could be much more than a friend. There's nothing unfair or dishonest about that, is there?"

"Not when you put it that way. Though I can't

say I see myself as 'compelling.' I'm just *me*," he said gruffly.

Pippi smiled. "Believe it or not, you are pretty special. And Mary's bound to realize that eventually. We're just trying to make sure it happens sooner instead of later." She paused. "That's why I've decided to go ahead and give you dancing lessons. But don't you dare use your fancy tricks on me ever again!"

"Right. Except, of course, when I'm just practicing."

Pippi gritted her teeth. There was no "of course" about it. She didn't want him using those tricks on her *at all!* But he didn't give her a chance to disagree.

"Shall I come over tomorrow night at the same time?" he asked.

"No! I mean, tomorrow night isn't convenient." She had to have more time to prepare herself for the ordeal. Tomorrow was much too soon.

"Oh, I see." His voice suddenly became flat and expressionless. "No doubt you and Marc have something already planned?"

Before Pippi could bring herself to imply a lie by nodding in agreement, Jeremy asked another question. "Does Marc know I'm here tonight?"

"Um . . . no," she answered. At least *that* wasn't a lie, though she was uncomfortably aware that it left out most of the truth.

"I suppose you were afraid he might feel jealous. After all, you and I both know that my visit has been completely innocent, but he might not realize that."

"Listen, why don't I call you?" she suggested, frantically eager to end this awkward conversation. "We can set up a time for the dance lessons after we've both looked at our schedules. Okay?"

"Okay." Jeremy stood up and headed for the door, stopping by the coatrack to retrieve his jacket. His back was toward Pippi as he shrugged the coat on over his broad shoulders. When he turned to face her once more, his expression had softened.

"I appreciate what you're trying to do for me, Pip," he said quietly. "I just hope it works."

Pippi stared at him in silence. How could it *not* work? What woman in her right mind could resist Jeremy Holt if he courted her in earnest?

"Don't worry. It'll work," she reassured him.

"We'll see." He gave her a wry smile and opened the door. "Good night, Pip."

His voice seemed to leave tiny echoes in the room as the door closed behind him. The air still vibrated with the husky cadence of those three words of farewell.

"Damn," Pippi muttered as the realization struck. "He's practicing on me again!"

Three

The phone was ringing in Pippi's apartment as she wrestled the wicker laundry basket up the last flight of stairs.

"Hello?" she panted after dropping the basket on the landing outside, unlocking her door, and barreling across the room to the phone. All in the space of three rings.

"Did I catch you in the shower again?" Even through the faint hum of the long-distance connection, the note of rueful amusement was evident in the caller's voice.

"Arri!" Pippi exclaimed with delight, using the nickname her sister preferred, not too surprisingly, to her given name of Arrietty. "It's great to hear from you! And no, I wasn't in the shower this time. Just lugging my clean laundry up the stairs."

"That's an improvement anyway. At least I'm not forcing you to drip water all over the floor. So tell me, what's new in snowy Minneapolis?"

"The snow's all melted. Finally. And I broke up

with Marc. Two nights ago." Pippi waited nervously to hear Arri's reaction to her blunt announcement.

"Is it over *for good* this time?" Arri asked skeptically. And hopefully.

"Of course it's over for good! No way would I take that slimy reptile back again after this!"

"Thank goodness!" her sister blurted out. "It's about time you opened your eyes and saw that guy for what he is! So, what did he do that finally made you see the light?"

"It was at an engagement party for some friends of mine, Bill and Joanne. I noticed that Marc was drinking a bit too much, so I tried to drop him a tactful hint. Well, he blew up. Right in the middle of the party he started calling me names. It was a nasty scene that embarrassed everybody—especially me!"

"How awful for you, Pippi."

"Wait. That's not all. He left the room in a huff and I figured I'd give him a chance to cool off. But when I went looking for him twenty minutes later, I found him trying to back Joanne into a corner, doing an imitation of an octopus. You know—all hands."

"That sounds like Marc all right."

"There's more, Arri. As soon as he saw me, he had the *nerve* to pretend that Joanne had been 'leading him on!' Even though it was obvious she'd been quietly struggling with him the whole time, trying to avoid another unpleasant public scene."

"So what happened *then*?"

"My sweet, quiet friend Joanne, who normally wouldn't hurt a flea, turned to me and said, 'Do I have your permission to slug him?' I said, 'Please do.' And she did."

"Bravo!"

"We got the guys to carry him out and drive him home, and after that we all had a wonderful time. But now I'm worried."

"Why? You just solved ninety-nine percent of your troubles the minute you got rid of Marc. So what's to worry about?"

"*Me!*" Pippi wailed. "Arri, there's got to be something wrong with me! Why can't I fall in love with a nice, normal guy and have a nice, normal relationship? No matter how hard I try, every time I fall in love it ends up in disaster!"

"Maybe it's just bad luck," her sister suggested doubtfully.

"No. If it had happened only once or twice, *that* could be considered bad luck. But three times is a definite trend! What am I doing wrong?"

"You're picking the wrong men to fall in love with," Arri bluntly informed her.

"That's what Jeremy said. In his opinion Stephen, Rob, and Marc were all alike!"

"He's right. They even *looked* sort of alike, which always freaked me out. And speaking of Jeremy, why do you keep falling for jerks when you've got that sexy, irresistible man just waiting to be fallen in love with?"

"You mean *Jeremy?*" Pippi asked incredulously.

"Of course I mean Jeremy! I didn't want to say anything before, when you were still hung up on Marc, but . . ." Arri paused portentously. "I think he's got a crush on you. Last time I was in Minneapolis your good friend Jeremy showed all the symptoms of a man truly smitten."

Something inside Pippi gave a startled, convulsive leap, then subsided into an oddly painful ache. She tried to laugh. "You're right, he *is* smitten . . . but not with me. It's just as well. He's not my type. Too shy."

"Are you kidding? He didn't seem at all shy to me. He was witty and fun and *nice.* And what's all this baloney about your 'type?' Did it ever occur to you that that might be your whole problem?"

Pippi held the receiver a little farther away from her ear as Arri's indignant voice went up a few decibels. "What do you mean?" she asked cautiously.

"It's obvious that your preconceptions keep steering you wrong, Pippi! Your type always seems to be the *wrong* type! So why don't you try being more open-minded? Give some of those other types a chance. Like Jeremy."

"I just told you, he's in love with another woman," Pippi said through clenched teeth. "Besides, I've got a better idea. From now on I'm not falling in love again with *anyone.* It's more trouble than it's worth."

"Oh, Pippi—" Arri began in a worried tone.

"Listen, there's somebody at the door," Pippi lied. "I'll call you in a couple of weeks, okay? 'Bye." She hung up the phone abruptly, and then promptly felt ashamed of herself.

Just because her sister's comments had been oddly upsetting was no excuse for lying and rudeness. Pippi knew she ought to call back right now and apologize. But what if her sister asked more probing questions? What if she kept mentioning Jeremy? For some reason just the thought made Pippi feel confused and apprehensive. So she didn't call back.

Later that afternoon she did force herself to call Jeremy. He was out, but she left a message on his answering machine. "Your first lesson at the Amazing Pippi Smith School of Dance and Etiquette has been scheduled for Tuesday evening at nine P.M. Tutus need not be worn."

•   •   •

Jeremy showed up promptly on Tuesday night, wearing dark slacks and an open-necked white cotton shirt. No tutu. But Pippi found herself staring nonetheless.

The shirt had no hint of a ruffle, yet somehow it made him look like a fair-haired, swashbuckling swordsman of the eighteenth century. Slim-waisted and agile, he had the same whiplike strength and swiftness as the long, slender steel of a duelling sword. But he was here for a dancing lesson, not a fencing match, Pippi reminded herself.

"I brought you something," he announced hesitantly, breaking the awkward silence. Belatedly, Pippi realized she'd kept him standing in the doorway while she gaped at him like an idiot. "It's not as romantic as flowers, I'm afraid, but . . ."

With a flourish he produced a sturdy aluminum stepladder from its hiding place just to the side of the door. "*Voilà*," he said as he carried it inside and set it up. "Or *viola*, as my kid sister used to say. Now you won't have to depend on anybody else to help you reach the top of your cupboard."

"That's the most thoughtful gift anyone's ever given me!" Pippi exclaimed, impulsively flinging her arms around his neck. Immediately, she became aware of the tension in him. The instant her body came in contact with his, his muscles went as taut as steel cables.

She hastily tried to draw away, but his arms suddenly tightened around her, trapping her against him. "I'm glad you like it," he said softly, gazing down into her confused blue eyes. A whimsical smile played at the corners of his mouth, and Pippi suddenly got the crazy notion that he was about to kiss her.

It didn't make sense. Why would he stiffen in obvious rejection one minute and then, the very next minute, start seductively caressing the small of her back as he was doing now? Why did the tender flame in his eyes send traitorous sparks shooting through her veins, when Jeremy was nothing more than a friend?

The gentle pressure of his fingertips on her lower back brought her even closer. She took a deep breath, inadvertently filling her nostrils with a subtle yet intoxicating blend of fragrances: the freshly laundered scent of his clean white shirt, the faint aroma of sandalwood soap, and Jeremy's own fresh masculinity.

She could feel the strong, flexed muscles of his arms and thighs as he held her against him. His smiling, persuasive mouth hovered mere inches from her own, and she suddenly realized that the last few threads of her common sense were coming unraveled. The voice inside her that had been asking "Why?" was suddenly asking "Why not?"

Pippi jerked out of Jeremy's arms and stepped away. She knew "why not!" Because Jeremy was only practicing again. That voice, that smile, that look in his eyes—they were all ultimately intended for someone else, not Pippi.

"Let's get one thing straight," she said in a choked voice. "From now on I don't want you practicing on me unless we've agreed to it ahead of time. If we're going to be playacting, I want to know we're playacting! All this switching back and forth without warning is confusing as hell."

"But I—"

"I mean it, Jeremy. I can't deal with it when my friend suddenly starts acting like my lover and then I have to quickly remind myself that it's all an act! That's too many emotional somersaults per second for me."

He looked thoroughly dismayed at her outburst. "Pip, I'm sorry. I had no idea . . ."

"Well, now you know how I feel. So please don't put on any more acts with me, except during our 'official' practice sessions."

"I'll try not to put on an act," he said quietly.

A short silence served to solemnize their agreement. Jeremy appeared to be deep in thought and Pippi wondered, uneasily, what he had on his mind. She hoped he wasn't speculating too closely on the reasons why his spur-of-the-moment playacting had upset her so much. It would be very embarrassing if he guessed how potent a reaction she had to all his "practicing."

"Are you ready for your first dancing lesson?" she asked quickly.

"As ready as I'll ever be. Where do you want me to put your new stepladder?"

"I think it'll fit into the broom closet in the kitchen. And Jeremy . . ." She put her hand on his arm and looked up at him. "It's a wonderful present. I'll never feel too short in my own kitchen again. Thank you."

"You're welcome." His mouth quirked and there was a slightly devilish glint in his eyes as his gaze dropped to where her hand possessed his arm. "It's funny, Pip, but if I didn't know better, I might accuse you of practicing some of those seductive tactics on me right this minute."

She yanked her hand away as if she'd been stung. "I am not! What a rotten thing to say!"

"But you *were* touching my arm and making eye contact. And you were using that meaningful, murmurous voice of yours to give a lot of emphasis to a simple thank-you. What's a poor guy supposed to think?" he said facetiously.

"You're supposed to think I'm sincerely grateful

for the stepladder. Period. And if you have the nerve to think anything else—"

"Whoa, Pip, whoa!" he said, laughing. "I *don't* think anything else. I was just trying to make a point."

"What point?"

"That it's not fair to jump to conclusions every time I use a certain tone of voice or look you right in the eye." As he was doing right this minute, Pippi noted. "We're friends, Pip. Shouldn't we be able to express our affection for each other without being accused of sharpening our mate-hunting tools?"

"I—I guess so." She gulped. He made it sound so logical, so reasonable. But Pippi had a feeling she was going to end up twice as confused as before. What if she couldn't tell the difference between a friendly show of affection and Jeremy's version of the come-hither voice and look? Already she kept getting pretense mixed up with reality. Who knew what might happen next?

But Jeremy seemed to have no qualms. "Now that *that's* settled, teach me to dance," he commanded as he folded the stepladder and carried it into the kitchen.

The rugs were rolled up and the furniture was pushed against the walls. Pippi noticed her hand was trembling as she knelt in front of the stereo and gently lowered the needle onto the first record she'd selected. She wasn't ready for this.

The pulsing, irresistible beat of the lively dance number filled the room. She stood up and turned to face Jeremy, who was standing in the center of the bare, gleaming floor. The sight of his taut, still figure did nothing to restore her confidence. He looked so intimidatingly large and male and muscular! Pippi's mouth went dry at the thought of brazenly placing herself in his arms.

But she *had* promised to teach him to dance. She surreptitiously wiped her damp palms on her plaid wool skirt and straightened the turtleneck of her soft midnight-blue sweater. She wished now that she'd worn jeans and a sweatshirt, but at the time this outfit had seemed more appropriate for dancing. She hadn't expected to feel quite so vulnerable with Jeremy.

"Ready when you are, Pip," he said with a grin that tried to be nonchalant but didn't quite make it. He wasn't as casual and relaxed about all this as he pretended to be, she realized. Holding someone in your arms and moving in time to music was a fairly intimate act, even if it was socially acceptable in public and wasn't supposed to mean a thing.

She tried to smile as she walked toward him. Her pulse was beating furiously and her breathing was quick and shallow. This was it.

"First, we'll work on the correct position," she said in a resolute, if slightly breathless voice. "Take your right hand and put it on my back, here, right below my shoulder blade. Good." She was determined to ignore the delicious and disturbing sensations that emanated from the firm touch of his open palm against her back.

"Now I rest my left hand here on your shoulder." Her voice quivered as she felt the warmth of his flesh and the hard contours of his muscles through the thin fabric of his shirt. "And then you clasp my right hand in your left, like this."

Gently, his fingers gripped hers, and they stood face to face. The seconds seemed to last forever as she looked up into his intent brown eyes. She could feel his quick breath stirring the curls at the side of her face.

"What's next, Teach?" he asked softly.

"Uh, I think I'd better show you the basic step you'll be using," she said, hastily twirling out of his hold so that they were standing side by side. "Just watch my feet."

She had him repeat the step several times, counting out the rhythm as he did so, and then she had him try to match his steps to the music. He seemed to get the hang of it very swiftly. All too soon for Pippi's peace of mind, it was time to assume their dancing position once more.

"Let's see if I can remember where to put my hands," Jeremy said as they faced each other. Pippi could have sworn that his mischievous gaze lingered a moment too long on the soft fullness of her breasts, so evident beneath the clinging sweater. But his hand went to its proper place on her back, just above the curve of her waist. Maybe she'd imagined that brief, suggestive glance.

But she knew she wasn't imagining her body's reaction. Her nipples stirred to hardness and her cheeks flushed bright rose. Her hand trembled as Jeremy wrapped it in the warm clasp of his.

He gave her a questioning look as he became aware of the tremor in her flesh where it came in contact with his. "Are you afraid I'm going to stomp on your feet?" he teased gently.

"Yes, *terrified*," she said, trying to make a joke of it. It was a relief to hear Jeremy's answering laughter.

"I promise I'll be very careful." Then he steered her lightly out onto the broad expanse of uncarpeted floor, and they began to dance.

Pippi was overwhelmed by sensory impressions. Like a swirling flock of birds with beating wings, those impressions invaded her consciousness, leaving her dazed and confused. The music throbbed in her ears as the blood throbbed in her veins. Each time she breathed she absorbed the subtle, exciting scent of Jeremy's nearness. Her hand on his shoulder transmitted to her brain each disturbing ripple of his firm, muscled body. And the skin on her back felt imprinted with a burning, detailed awareness of the hand that held her.

It wasn't until Jeremy made a false step, interrupting the flowing, rhythmic movement of their bodies, that Pippi suddenly recalled that she had a task to perform. She wasn't supposed to be mindlessly drifting along in Jeremy's arms—she had promised to teach him to dance.

"You've been doing very well," she said in her most schoolmarmish voice. "Now I think it's time to work on some variations and additional moves."

She concentrated so hard on teaching and executing the new steps that after a while she forgot to be self-conscious about the constant physical contact between Jeremy and herself. They were simply partners in a challenging athletic endeavor. If she was flushed and breathless, it was due to physical exertion, nothing more.

"Oops!" Jeremy exclaimed as their latest maneuver ended in an awkward collision. Flung off balance by the impact of their bodies, Pippi clutched at his shoulder for support and found herself draped against his chest, trying to regain her footing.

Her husky, breathless laughter broke loose as soon as her eyes met Jeremy's. "You're a menace!" she accused him. "You learn so fast that I keep forgetting you're just a beginner, and *then* you get your feet tangled up, right when I least expect it!"

"That's because I got carried away and started

thinking I was Fred Astaire." He grinned. "I never knew dancing could be so much fun."

"Well, you certainly seem to have a natural talent for it. In fact, I think you're ready for your big night on the town with Mary, as of now. You don't need any more lessons from me."

He looked aghast. "No, Pip! I *do* need more lessons!" he protested. "I'll be hopeless without them."

Pippi felt a rush of tenderness at this sudden return of Jeremy's shy, vulnerable side. "Have a little faith in yourself," she admonished him softly. "It's only natural to be nervous, but I know you can do it. After just one lesson you're already as good a dancer as most men could ever hope to be."

"I'm not ready," he insisted grimly.

"Yes, you are. Come on. Let's dance some more, and you'll see I'm right."

But the dancing did not go very smoothly after that. Suddenly, Jeremy seemed to be tripping over his own feet. He made his turns in the wrong direction. He started counting under his breath, and then missed the beat. His hold on Pippi became cramped and awkward.

If there had been any other dancers present, Pippi had no doubt that he would have bumped into them. On purpose, of course. By the time his foot landed squarely across her instep, she was no longer amused.

"Listen, you big moron! I know you're doing this deliberately! But your little acts of sabotage are *not* going to change my mind, so you might as well quit before you break a leg. *No more lessons.*"

"Are you implying that I—" He stopped short as he caught the full impact of her warning glare, and his overdone expression of astonishment and wounded innocence gave way to an unabashed grin. He shrugged. "It seemed worth a try."

"Well, it wasn't. It was feeble and pathetically obvious." She knew the corners of her mouth were tweaking upward even as she spoke. It was impossible to stay mad at Jeremy for very long.

"Thanks." His impudent smile slowly faded into seriousness. "So, this is my last dancing lesson. What do you say we make the most of it while we can?"

Without waiting for her response he pulled her into his arms and swept her up in the languorous, sentimental mood of the tune that poured out of the stereo speakers. There was no stumbling now as they glided across the floor like swans on a lake, or like comets streaking across the night sky.

He held her close, closer than in any previous dance. Their bodies spoke and understood a language that had no words as they moved intimately together in shared rhythm. They were like opposite sides of a spinning coin, joined as one in a shifting, swirling, shimmering pattern of synchronized motion.

Pippi looked up at Jeremy and felt a hollow, dizzy sensation in the pit of her stomach. His face was glowing with excitement and rapt concentration. At this moment he belonged only to her and to the music. And Pippi was shocked to realize how much that pleased her.

But before she had time to examine this unwelcome realization too closely, she became aware that someone was knocking at her front door. *Pounding* on it, actually, in order to be heard over the music.

"Were you expecting anyone?" Jeremy asked. His expression was stern. "Marc, perhaps?"

"No. Would you mind turning down the music while I see who it is?"

It was Mrs. Walters, her neighbor from the apartment below. Wearing an old bathrobe and with her hair up in curlers, Mrs. Walters managed to look both apologetic and indignant. As soon as Jeremy had lowered the volume on the stereo, she rushed into speech.

"Miss Smith," she began, "I hate to complain, but I can't get to sleep with all this noise going on up here. Not only has the music been blaring, but what sounds like a herd of buffalo has been trampling back and forth across my ceiling!"

"I'm sorry, Mrs. Walters," Pippi said, hiding her amusement. "My friend and I were just practicing our dance steps."

"But it's after eleven! And you know how early I have to get up to go to work. Couldn't you please—"

"Omigosh! I had no idea it was so late! Mrs. Walters, I *am* sorry. We won't be dancing anymore tonight, I promise!"

After bidding good night to a mollified Mrs. Walters, Pippi shut the door and turned around to find Jeremy grinning at her.

"A whole herd of buffalo, huh?" He shook his head. "So much for my illusion that we were dancing on air."

Something in his voice made her pulse start to flutter, but Pippi just laughed. "No, we were dancing on Mrs. Walters's ceiling."

As quickly and quietly as possible they unrolled the rugs and moved the furniture back into place. Late though it was, Pippi decided to offer Jeremy a beer, and she wasn't surprised when he accepted eagerly. After all, dancing was thirsty work, and so was moving furniture.

"I've been thinking, Pip," he said, taking a swig

of the cold beer and leaning back against the sofa cushions.

"That's unusual," Pippi murmured, watching the graceful rippling of his throat muscles as he swallowed.

He lobbed a pillow across the coffee table at her, then turned serious again. "You say I'm ready for my big date with Mary, yet I don't *feel* ready. But I just realized, it's not the dancing I'm worried about now. It's everything else."

"What do you mean?"

"I've never taken anybody out for this kind of an evening before. I don't know what to wear, where to go, or how to act when I get there! You've got to help me, Pip!"

"I'll be happy to give you all the advice you need, Jeremy."

"I need more than advice, Pip. I need a dress rehearsal. Please, come dancing with me on Friday night and show me the ropes. Make suggestions. Tell me if I'm doing anything wrong."

"But—"

"*Please*, Pip. I've got to build up my confidence somehow, and you're my only hope."

That did it. Who could turn down an appeal like that? Not Pippi. Not when her best friend needed her so desperately. And it was simply absurd to feel uneasy about spending more time alone with him. He was only Jeremy, after all.

"Sure, why not?" she said with a smile.

Four

Afterward, Pippi wondered at what point Friday evening's events had veered out of her control. Personally, she blamed the gypsy violinist, but that was probably unfair. After all, the trouble had already started by then. She should never have agreed to go out dancing with Jeremy in the first place. And she should never, *ever* have agreed to follow *his* ground rules for the evening!

"Of course you realize what this means?" he'd said as soon as she consented to his suggestion of a Friday night "dress rehearsal" for his big date with Mary.

"Of course. It means I need my head examined," Pippi replied ruefully.

"Wrong. It means that Friday night will be one long official practice session," he proclaimed gleefully. "I'm giving you fair warning that I'll be rehearsing every trick you've taught me."

"Absolutely not."

"Absolutely yes! From the minute I arrive to escort you to dinner, to the minute I k—"

Pippi had stopped listening the second he said *dinner*. "Whoa!" she cried. "I never said I'd have *dinner* with you! We're just going out dancing, remember?"

"Oh, no, Pip. I've got this all figured out. My first real date with the woman I love has got to be an evening so romantic, she'll remember it for the rest of her life. I'm going to do everything in my power to make her fall in love with me. And I've decided to start things off with a candlelight dinner at the best restaurant in town."

Thoroughly taken aback to hear this solemn, resolute declaration coming from shy, bashful Jeremy Holt, Pippi stared at him a full ten seconds before replying.

"That's not a bad idea," she said. "But I doubt if you need any practice taking a woman out to dinner, Jeremy. So I'll pass on that part of the evening if you don't mind." She managed to dredge up the ghost of her usual husky laugh.

"You don't understand. I've got to practice the whole thing, from beginning to end. That's the only way I'll know if I can make it work. And I need your criticism and advice every step of the way."

Pippi felt as if she'd blundered into a giant, sticky spiderweb, and now the silken strands were tightening around her. "But—" she began.

"I know it's asking a lot, Pip," he said anxiously. "The whole evening's likely to be a total bore for you."

She had to smile. Boredom was dead last on her list of worries at the moment. But maybe she was blowing things all out of proportion. Maybe the evening *would* turn out to be rather tedious. And she did owe Jeremy all the help she could give.

"Okay, I'll be your guinea pig," she said.

It was no surprise that Jeremy looked exceedingly elegant when he showed up at Pippi's door on the big night. After all, they'd had more than one lengthy telephone consultation about what he should wear. Pippi ought to have been prepared. But she took one look at the disturbingly handsome man on her doorstep and felt like running for cover.

How was she supposed to keep her head for an entire evening of being wined, dined, wooed, and courted by a man who looked like *that?* She mustn't forget, not even for one second, that tonight was all make-believe.

She herself had dressed for the occasion with great care—or, it might be more accurate to say, with great caution. No bare shoulders, no low-cut neckline, and no body-hugging fit. But the simply styled silk dress with its high mandarin collar and cap sleeves was one of her favorites. It was the same deep shade of blue as woodsmoke seen against snowy hills on a winter evening, and it brought out the blue depths of her eyes and the flaming sunset tints of her hair.

"You look magnificent," Jeremy said softly, and Pippi felt the nape of her neck tingle at the warm, exciting caress of his velvety tones.

"You don't look too shabby yourself." There was a dry, ironic edge to her voice.

"Thanks." As he helped her on with her lightweight wool wrap, his hands briefly touched her shoulders, sending a wave of awareness through her body.

"Where did you learn *that* trick?" she asked lightly. "It wasn't one that I taught you."

"It just seemed to come naturally." His eyes were

bright with amusement, but his voice held a hint of something more. "After all, I'm not totally ignorant in these matters. I haven't been hiding under a rock for the last ten years."

"But you do spend a lot of time alone with your computer, buried under a stack of income tax forms! In fact, I hardly saw you at all last month. Not until after the fifteenth anyway."

"Most accountants do put in a little overtime in April," he dryly reminded her.

"Excuses, excuses!" Pippi responded with a saucy grin. "So, are we going to stand here talking all night, or are you going to show me a good time?"

"Lady, I'm going to show you the most romantic evening ever planned by a certified public accountant!"

She gave a most unladylike snort and opened her mouth to speak. But then she shut it again, shaking her head. "Naw, too easy. I've got way too much class to make any of the obvious insulting remarks you're expecting to hear."

"Whew! That sure takes a load off my mind!" He wiped some imaginary drops of perspiration from his brow. "Grab your bowling shoes and that twofer-one coupon for the hot dog stand, and let's go!"

Pippi had to be helped down the stairs, because she was laughing so hard. And when they finally reached the bottom, Jeremy drew out his trusty Irish linen handkerchief and proceeded to dry her tears of mirth.

The touch of his fingers on her cheek stilled her laughter. He gently dabbed at her eyelids with the soft fabric, blotting up the salty moisture that had beaded her lashes.

"You've made me cry again, you brute," she teased, but her voice sounded shaky, and she knew it wasn't just from laughter. His touch wove a bewitching tapestry of tiny but intense sensations across the delicate skin of her face.

"My apologies," he murmured in a bemused tone. He gazed down at her so intently that Pippi was afraid he could read in her face all the confusion she felt each time he touched her.

"Shall we go?" she prompted awkwardly.

"Of course." His nod gave the impression of a courtly bow. "My lady, your carriage awaits." Taking her arm with great formality, he escorted her out the door.

Pippi's glance darted up and down the block, searching for Jeremy's unflashy but well-designed and expensive little European car—an eminently suitable automobile for a successful young accountant, she'd always thought. "Where'd you park?" she asked, puzzled.

"Right in plain sight." He swept his arm toward the curb with a grand flourish.

"Omigosh," Pippi muttered in disbelief as her brain finally registered the fact that a gleaming cream-colored Rolls-Royce was parked in front of her house. Its sophisticated elegance made all the houses and cars on the street look shabby by comparison.

"Do you like it?" Jeremy asked eagerly.

"Please, please, *please* tell me you weren't cuckoo enough to put yourself in debt for the rest of your life by actually buying that gorgeous, impractical pile of metal!" she pleaded.

He frowned, disguising the twinkling gleam in his eye. "Well, I did consider it. And if I had bought it, I estimate I could have paid off the loan in exactly four point five years—hardly a lifetime debt. But after I'd weighed my options, I decided it was more cost effective just to rent it for the occasion."

"Accountants!" She rolled her eyes in disgust. "You'd better not talk that way to Mary, or she'll be convinced you don't have a romantic bone in your body. Tell me, have you *ever* done anything on impulse, without thinking it out beforehand?"

"Oh, yes." He smiled a tender, reminiscent smile. "The day I fell in love was like that. It happened so fast I never got the chance to make an analytical, objective, informed decision."

"Does that bother you?" she asked curiously as he led her down the front walk. She found it difficult to picture Jeremy letting himself be swept away by pure emotion.

"Not at all." He unlocked the passenger door of the Rolls and then turned to face her. His keen eyes looked steadily into hers, and the deep-timbred sureness of his voice sent an inexplicable shiver down her spine. "You see, I've had plenty of time to think it over since then, and I've reached the conclusion that my instincts were one hundred percent correct. This woman is the one for me."

"So now all you have to do is convince her that you're the one for her." Pippi felt an odd little ache in the pit of her stomach at the thought of the unknown woman who had slipped past all Jeremy's logic, sneaked straight into his heart, and found such a warm, tender welcome there.

Why couldn't it have been me? a tiny voice whispered. The unspoken words reverberated in her brain, and Pippi felt a chill of horror. How could her own thoughts betray her that way? She wanted that insane, impossible wish to disappear back to where it had come from. She wanted those words to be erased from her brain. Of course she hadn't meant . . . Of course not. It was silly to fly into a panic over one absurd little slip of the brain waves.

"Watch out for the orchids!" Jeremy shouted.

"Orchids?" Her shoulders were suddenly, violently, gripped by a pair of strong hands that prevented her body from observing the usual laws of gravity. Another fraction of a second and her rear end would have come to rest on the plushly upholstered seat of the Rolls-Royce. But that spot was already occupied by a white carton.

"Sorry, Pip," Jeremy said, holding her frozen in midair with one hand while his other hand snaked under her to rescue the florist's box. "I should have remembered to give you this earlier."

As she was released from his grasp, Pippi sank breathlessly, bonelessly, against the cushioned seat. Her heart was still racing a mile a minute, and her expression was dazed as she looked down at the box he placed in her lap, then up again at Jeremy.

"Are you okay?" he asked, concerned. "Did I hurt you when I grabbed you so hard?" She shook her head. Thank goodness he had no idea what crazy thoughts and desires had been churning inside her during the past few seconds.

He closed her door and hurried around to the driver's side. He looked flustered all to pieces as he climbed into the car.

"If you're this nervous just for the rehearsal, I hate to think what you'll be like with Mary," Pippi teased, hoping to ease the tension in the air.

Jeremy's face was nearly unreadable in the dim, shadowed interior of the Rolls, but Pippi saw the white gleam of his teeth when he grinned. "Now you see how right I was about needing practice!" he said. "I can't even present a corsage to a lady without accidentally manhandling her in the process."

"Why bother with a corsage at all? This isn't the senior prom."

"It's all part of the romantic evening, Pip," he replied a trifle reproachfully. He switched on the overhead light. "Go ahead, open the box."

She did, and carefully lifted out the delicate, fragile arrangement of blooms that had been nestled in tissue paper inside. They were so lovely she wanted to cry.

When she didn't say a word Jeremy peered at her anxiously. "Don't you like them?"

"Oh, yes. They're very beautiful. But . . ." She didn't know a tactful way to express the fear that was suddenly tugging at her heart.

"But what?"

"Nothing. Just . . . how's Mary going to react to all this? First a Rolls-Royce and now orchids! It's all pretty overwhelming for a first date, don't you think?"

"But don't I *want* to overwhelm her? Isn't that what this whole plan of yours is all about?"

"But it's *you* she should be overwhelmed by, Jeremy! Not by a lot of outrageously expensive trimmings! Not by the things your money can buy."

He stared at her for a second, open-mouthed, and then burst into laughter. "I don't believe this! You're trying to warn me that the woman I love could turn out to be a gold digger, right?"

Pippi squirmed uncomfortably. "I wouldn't put it quite like that," she muttered. "But it's no laughing matter. There *are* women who judge a man solely by the size of his wallet, and if you start trying to impress people by throwing your cash around, that's the kind of woman you're likely to attract."

She was afraid her plain speaking might anger

him, but she saw only amusement and affection in the glance he gave her. "You're forgetting that Mary and I are good friends. I know her too well to have any worries like that. Believe me, she couldn't care less how much money I have."

"As long as you're sure of that."

"I am." His quiet voice brooked no argument, but still an elusive twinkle danced in his eyes.

So that was that. She couldn't very well tell Jeremy she doubted his judgment when it came to the mysterious woman who had so quickly and completely wrapped him around her finger. But Pippi was worried nonetheless.

Jeremy and his partner, Larry Sommers, operated one of the most successful accounting firms in the Twin Cities. Though neither man was over thirty-five, they had established quite a dazzling reputation as financial consultants and tax planners for scores of prominent people and thriving businesses. Pippi had no idea what Jeremy's annual income was; she just knew it was a lot.

And that would qualify him as a very desirable meal ticket indeed in the eyes of some women. Pippi feared that he was just shy and vulnerable enough to be taken in by somebody like that. She sighed and leaned back against the cushioned comfort of the Rolls-Royce. Who would have guessed that Jeremy would do something so absurd and touchingly romantic as rent a Rolls! She just hoped Mary appreciated her good fortune.

Champagne bubbles tickled Pippi's nose and she laughed. She was having a wonderful time. The food at this restaurant was the best she'd ever eaten, and Jeremy was the nicest, funniest, handsomest— But no. She had to stop thinking thoughts like that. They'd only get her into trouble.

"May I have a bite of your scampi?" Jeremy asked with a coaxing smile that made Pippi feel quite dizzy. "I'll trade you some of my stuffed lobster tail."

She nodded, and before she knew what he was up to, he had leaned forward and lifted a generous forkful of the lobster until it was within two inches of her mouth. Its savory scent rose enticingly to her nostrils, and her lips parted almost of their own accord. Jeremy placed the succulent morsel in her mouth.

Pippi was keenly aware of his gaze warming her face as she tried to concentrate on the taste and texture of the food she was chewing. She lowered her eyes self-consciously.

"You've got a little speck of sauce on your face," he said, smiling as his thumb lightly rubbed away the tiny smudge at the corner of her mouth. "There, it's gone. Now, where's that bite of scampi you promised me?"

Her lips were still tingling from his touch and her hand was trembling as she speared a large piece of shrimp and offered it up to his waiting mouth. She felt the slight tug on the fork as his teeth pulled the shrimp from the tines. She stared in bemused fascination at the subtle play of his jaw muscles as he chewed. When his tongue flicked out and appreciatively licked the curve of his upper lip, Pippi tore her gaze away. This was crazy.

"See, that's another trick I know about that you forgot to teach me," he said with a complacent smile. "It works pretty well, don't you think?"

She stared at him in shock. Did he have no idea what he was doing to her? Couldn't he *see*? Yet she must hope that his careless blindness to her feelings would continue. Otherwise, how could she ever look him in the eye again?

"Of course, it works even better with finger food," he added jovially. "Here, I'll show you." Quick as lightning he tore off a bite-size piece of the hot roll he had just buttered and reached across the table with the obvious intention of popping it into her mouth.

"No!" she protested, but the syllable was no sooner out of her mouth than she found her lips closing over not only the piece of roll but also the thumb and forefinger that held it.

"Mmm," Jeremy murmured with pleasure as his fingertip traced the moist inner edge of her lips. "See how much fun it is? Why don't you try it on me now?" His thumb brushed the warm fullness of her lower lip in a final caress, then withdrew.

"I'd rather not, thank you," she said weakly. She refused to look at him until she could be sure her face would not betray the hopeless desire his teasing touch evoked. "After all, I'm not the one who claims to need practice at this sort of thing," she reminded him.

"Ah, but if you're already so good at it, then it's practically your duty to show me your expert technique!" So saying, he gently grasped her hand, placed another piece of the buttered roll between her fingers, and lifted her hand to his mouth.

Pippi shut her eyes in anguished delight as his wet, silken mouth possessed her fingertips. His tongue tasted them. His teeth gnawed softly, yet fiercely at them, and he growled deep in his throat.

"Jeremy!" She snatched her hand away. "What are people going to think if they see you munching on my fingers and making animal noises?"

"They might think we were in love," he suggested with a whimsical smile. "But I doubt if they'll see us at all, since the lighting in this restaurant is practically nonexistent." He reached for her hand again, but Pippi was too quick for him this time.

"That's enough of *that.* I'd like to eat the rest of my dinner before it gets cold, and I'd just as soon eat it without any help from you."

"You take away all my fun," he said with mock plaintiveness. "Oh, well, my next surprise for the evening is due to arrive any minute now." He glanced at his watch. "In fact, he's already ten minutes late."

"*He?* Another surprise? Jeremy, I'm not sure I can *take* another surprise!"

"You'll love it. It's the most romantic gesture I could come up with on such short notice."

"Now, why doesn't that reassure me?" Pippi questioned in a fatalistic voice, gazing up at the ceiling.

Just then the headwaiter approached their table, looking about as flustered as a headwaiter may permit himself to look. "Sir, there is a . . . gentleman out front who claims he's been hired by *you* to perform on these premises."

"Good. Have him begin as soon as he's tuned up."

"But sir—"

"And here's a little something for the inconvenience to you and your staff."

A "little something" indeed! The glimpse she caught of the size of the bill that changed hands made Pippi's toes curl.

"Yes, sir." The man bowed his head respectfully and seemed to melt away into the shadows.

Pippi turned to Jeremy with a look of wry amusement. "Pretty suave," she teased. "But my advice is to take care of that kind of cash transaction ahead of time when you come here with Mary. It looks a lot smoother that way."

"Yes, Teach," he said meekly. "I meant to get it all arranged earlier, but I was so distracted and bewitched by the pleasure of your company that it completely slipped my mind."

Pippi stiffened. "You'd better save lines like that for Mary."

"But I have to try them out on you first to see if they work." He grinned. "That one was obviously a dud."

"Obviously." She attacked the food on her plate with grim determination. She knew Jeremy was watching her, but she refused to look up.

"Pippi." His voice was low and resonant, a velvety sound that stroked and smoothed her ruffled temper. "Don't be mad." He captured her left hand and cupped it tenderly between his large, slightly calloused palms. And then it began.

Violin music. Pouring into the dimly lit room, it permeated the air with a rich, full-bodied sweetness so intense that Pippi felt as if her bones were liquefying into honey. The music's haunting sensuality pierced her, enthralled her, and claimed her. Her hand, pressed tightly between Jeremy's, throbbed with awareness. Her eyes were drawn to his face and what she saw there gave her the sensation of tumbling down the side of a mountain. *He felt it too!* All the passion of the music was reflected in his turbulent brown eyes.

For two or three crazy seconds Pippi's world tilted upside down and whirled deliriously out of control. Then she thudded back to earth. Obviously, it was all a mistake. What she'd seen in Jeremy's eyes were his feelings for the absent Mary. Those feelings had nothing to do with his friend Pippi.

She pulled her hand free of his grasp and tried to pretend nothing had happened. She just about succeeded, but only because the violinist happened to end his song just then. A pattering of startled applause broke out around the restaurant and Pippi clapped, too, as if that were the only reason she'd drawn her hand away from Jeremy's.

Her eyes carefully avoided him by seeking out a glimpse of the musician who had wrought such aural magic. To her surprise, he turned out to be a short, swarthy, oddly dressed man with a gold earring in one ear.

"What do you think of my surprise?" Jeremy asked softly.

Of course. She should have guessed that this was Jeremy's "romantic gesture." And she could certainly attest that it *was* romantic. But she wasn't about to let Jeremy know that the combination of him and the music was so potent, it had almost knocked her off her feet.

"He plays very well," she said in a matter-of-fact voice. "Where did you find him?"

"Playing on a downtown street corner, passing the hat for nickels and dimes."

"You're kidding. With all that talent? How sad."

"He claims he likes the freedom of that sort of Gypsy lifestyle. I don't know what he does in winter—maybe gets a regular job or heads for a warmer climate. But I'm glad he agreed to play for us tonight. He didn't seem too impressed by all the money I offered him, but when I told him I needed his music to win the heart of a woman, he couldn't resist the challenge."

"But, Jeremy! Isn't he going to think it's a bit odd when you hire him again in a few days to 'win the heart' of *another* woman?"

"Perhaps." Jeremy shrugged and grinned mischievously. "He's more likely to assume I'm just a fickle playboy and not think anything of it. Little does he know I'm a one-woman man."

Pippi felt a twinge of pain at his words. A one-woman man. What would it be like to have the steadfast love of such a man? That was something she'd never experienced, not even in her marriage. Especially not in her marriage. Dammit, did this Mary person have any idea how lucky she was?

All through coffee, dessert, and after-dinner liqueurs, Jeremy's Gypsy violinist continued to play. Pippi did her best not to lose her head, but in the end, what good was a head all stuffed with shimmering, silvery moonbeams? There was scarcely a rational thought in her brain after the music, the champagne, the candlelight, the liqueurs, and Jeremy's beguiling smiles had had their way with her.

As they were leaving the restaurant, he once again helped her on with her wrap, but this time his hands lingered on her shoulders, moving in a tentative caress. And then he lowered his head and kissed the back of her neck.

Pippi felt a plume of flame spring up in her loins as his mouth made intimate contact with her sensitive flesh. Vaguely, she knew she ought to protest, but she couldn't remember why. When Jeremy lifted his head and gently turned her around to face him, it was his eyes, dark and full of questions, that recalled her to a sense of her own peril. Even as mesmerized as she was, she knew better than to let him suspect how much that one little kiss had affected her.

"You've got great technique," she said just a trifle breathlessly. "But you mustn't come on too strong too fast. Remember, the whole point of taking Mary dancing is to get physically close to her *without* having to make any obvious moves. And kissing her on the neck is pretty obvious."

"I guess I got carried away," he said penitently. "What would I do without you to steer me right, Pip?"

"You'd manage," she said, and realized it was true. Jeremy was far from helpless when it came to women. He *was* shy and vulnerable and caring, but those very qualities gave him an added appeal. And a man as handsome and sexy and amusing as Jeremy didn't need much added appeal to be downright irresistible!

He put his hand on her waist as they walked to the car. "*This* is permissible, don't you think?" he asked, giving her ribs a gentle squeeze.

"Well . . ." Her voice trembled as she tried to ignore the spasm of delight provoked by his touch. "A casual hand at the waist is acceptable, but don't start squeezing her the way you're squeezing me. It's too suggestive."

"I'll try to remember that. Too bad I didn't bring a notebook to keep track of all these details."

Pippi shot him a sharp, suspicious glance. If he was laughing at her . . . But his face was poker-straight, the expression in his eyes bland and innocent.

The smoky, sensuous strains of dance music were weaving their way out the door and up into the fading twilight glow of the spring evening when Jeremy and Pippi arrived at the night spot he'd selected for the dancing portion of their "dress rehearsal."

Pippi felt a tingling awareness—an anticipation and a fear—as Jeremy took her arm and led her inside. It was almost here, the moment she'd been dreading, yet dreaming of, all evening. The moment when Jeremy would wrap his arms around her and make her forget everything but him and the rhythm that united them as one. Soon they would be dancing.

For a man who claimed to be inexperienced at such outings, Jeremy handled the technical details with incredible ease. Within minutes he had checked her wrap, found them a table, and ordered drinks.

Pippi took a gulp of the ginger ale she had requested, and wondered if she should have asked for black coffee. She felt thoroughly intoxicated in a way that had little to do with alcohol. Her stomach must surely have been invaded by a flock of hovering, darting hummingbirds. And her brain was still awash with slippery, sliding moonbeams.

When Jeremy stood up, smiling, and held out his hand to her, her legs went weak. His fingers felt hot as they clasped her ice-cold wrist. All the imaginary hummingbirds inside her went wild at his touch.

They walked to the dance floor, then turned and faced each other. "Do you remember everything I taught you?" she asked, trying valiantly to restore her sense of control over the situation.

"Everything, Pip," he murmured fervently in that voice that was deep and pungent, yet sweet as herb-flavored honey. "And this is what I've been waiting for all night—the chance to take you in my arms and feel your soft curves embracing me."

He's only rehearsing, so don't go getting all stirred up, she firmly ordered herself. It was good advice, but she completely ignored it nonetheless.

The glow in Jeremy's eyes was like a form of radiant energy that kissed her face as he gazed down at her. His left hand closed over her trembling fingers and his right hand splayed across her back like a fiery brand. Pippi sighed as she brought her left hand up to rest on his broad shoulder. Slowly, savoringly, Jeremy drew her unresisting body close against his muscled chest and thighs.

They danced. Even amid the surrounding crowd of moving, swaying couples, Pippi felt enfolded with Jeremy in a magic cloak of intimacy. Everywhere that his body touched hers through the thin silk of her dress, ripples of wildfire coursed over her skin. She was filled with impossible desire. It ebbed and flowed within her like the pulsing beat of the music.

Their moments together on the dance floor seemed timeless. Later, Pippi couldn't have said whether they danced for hours or mere minutes. All she knew was that she never wanted it to end. Yet, at the same time, she hoped she never had to undergo such exquisitely cruel torment ever again.

She was like a hungry beggar at a feast who was allowed to take one bite from every dish but was forbidden to swallow. She could taste the ambrosial sweetness of Jeremy's loving desire, but its nourishment wasn't hers to keep. And that left a gnawing hunger, a growing emptiness, deep inside her.

In the dark interior of the Rolls, driving home, Jeremy let the fingers of his right hand rest on the nape of Pippi's neck. The silken curtain of her hair brushed lightly against his knuckles.

"Damn," he muttered. "I should have had the sense to hire a chauffeur along with this car. That way you and I could have ridden home in the privacy of the backseat, entwined in each other's arms."

"There's still time, if you'd like to do that for your

date with Mary," Pippi reminded him in a quiet, lifeless voice. "After all, this is only a rehearsal."

Jeremy made no reply, but he took the corner onto her street a little more sharply than usual. She didn't notice. She was too busy wondering if Cinderella had felt this lousy, coming home with her dress turning back into rags and her coach back into a pumpkin.

Jeremy pulled into an empty parking space at the curb and braked the car to an abrupt halt.

"Well," Pippi said with artificial briskness, "other than a couple of weak spots that need work, tonight was devastatingly romantic. Mary's going to love it." Her fingers groped for the handle of the door behind her.

"Is that all you've got to say?"

His quiet question made her chest ache with the weight of other things she might have said, might have done if she had been more to him than a stand-in for another woman. She looked up at the smooth line of his jaw profiled against the light of a nearby streetlamp, and she longed to reach out and stroke his cheek, his neck, his hair. She longed to bury her face against his shoulder and breathe deeply of his scent, feel the leashed power of his muscled flesh.

"We can discuss it in more detail tomorrow after racquetball, okay?" she suggested quickly.

"Sure. But what about the rest of our rehearsal tonight? Aren't you going to invite me up to your place for coffee or a nightcap or whatever?"

"Very funny, Jeremy. If Mary asks you in for *whatever*, I'm sure you'll do just fine without practicing it on me first! Good night." She opened the car door and put her foot outside.

"Wait." The softly spoken syllable lingered in the air and held her where she was, poised on the verge of escape. "If I can't practice 'whatever' with you, Pip, at least give me a chance to practice my manners. I'll walk you to your apartment."

"That won't be necess—" But he was out the door and around to her side of the car before she could even finish the sentence.

Wordlessly, she allowed herself to be assisted out of the Rolls and up the front walk. Jeremy stood by as she unlocked the outer door, then he followed her up the three narrow flights of stairs to her apartment. She was already inserting and turning the key to unlock her door when his hand closed over hers.

"There's one more dating ritual I'd like to practice," he said in a husky voice that made the tiny silken hairs on the back of her neck stand up.

In the split-second before she could guess his meaning, his lips took hers by surprise. His arms encircled her and she was too weak with pent-up longing to resist. His tongue stroked the soft inner curve of her lips, then slipped deep inside her mouth.

His hands moved down her back with the pressure of a sculptor's hands molding clay. It seemed to Pippi that her flesh was created anew by his touch.

And then, abruptly, it was over. Jeremy drew away and his arms released her. There was a moment of silence while he brought his ragged breathing under control.

"What do you think, Pip? Was that an appropriate good night kiss for the occasion?"

She lowered her lashes to hide the sudden tears that sprang into her unwary eyes. "We'll talk about it tomorrow," she said in a raw, strained voice. Before he could voice an objection, she darted into her apartment and closed the door in his face.

Five

Pippi had a lot of demons to exorcise the next morning during their racquetball game. She was a great believer in the therapeutic value of exercise, but after a half hour of hard, intensive athletic competition, she had to admit it didn't seem to be doing the trick today. And she was afraid she knew why.

The sight of Jeremy, half-naked and gleaming with sweat, swooping around the racquetball court with the swift grace of a hawk, was definitely not calculated to rid her of her most troubling demon of all.

She had paced her floor for an hour the night before, trying to come to grips with the awful truth. "You've got the hots for *Holt!*" she'd accused herself aloud.

"Brilliant deduction, my dear Watson," was her scathing, sarcastic reply to herself. "For a whole week now, you've been turning into hot corn meal mush every time the man comes near you, yet it's taken you this long to figure out you're physically attracted to him?"

" 'Physically attracted,' ha! Face it, kid. You want him so bad, it's gnawing at your heart like a hungry wolf."

There was no disputing the truth of that. Still, she tried to find a reassuring thought to cling to. "It's probably just a fleeting attraction, and it'll fade quicker than a rainbow," she told herself.

"Sure. And any day now pigs will sprout wings and fly away. Get your head out of the sand, Pippi Smith! You've got a real problem on your hands, and you'd better figure out what you're going to do about it!"

Pippi's acrimonious debate with herself might have gone on all night if Mrs. Walters from downstairs hadn't come up to complain that she couldn't sleep with Pippi pacing back and forth across her ceiling.

"It sounds like a bunch of soldiers marching around in combat boots," Mrs. Walters objected. "And I thought I heard voices . . ." She glanced suspiciously around the room, as if she suspected Pippi of concealing someone.

Pippi blushed. "I had the radio on," she lied. She hated to add another falsehood to this week's already reprehensibly high total, but darn it all, she couldn't have Mrs. Walters telling everybody that Pippi Smith was certifiably wacko! And that was exactly what would happen if she guessed that Pippi had been carrying on a conversation all alone in an empty room.

But maybe she *was* certifiably wacko. That thought occurred to her now as she showered and changed after racquetball. Why else would she find herself suddenly pining over a man who was in love with someone else, after months of nothing but a

platonic friendship? Except for that one embarrassing night six months earlier, she had thought
of Jeremy only as a friend. So why did these feelings have to plague her *now*, just when it was
unthinkable for her to indulge in them?

By the time they sat down to a late breakfast at
their usual spot, Pippi thought she had things
under control. She was determined not to get into
any more situations where she would be left
exposed and vulnerable to Jeremy's unconscious
physical appeal.

All that grim resolve made her sound very crisp
and detached as she launched into a minutely
detailed catalog of every fault and flaw in Jeremy's
"rehearsal" performance the previous evening. By
the time she wound up her list of picky criticisms,
he looked miserable.

"Obviously, the evening was a total flop," he said
in a strained, unhappy voice.

"How can you say that?" she exclaimed, amazed.
"I already told you that the evening as a whole was
breathtakingly romantic. There were just a couple
of little things that needed work."

"But if last night was really as romantic as all
that, you wouldn't be sitting here giving me this
carping, cold-blooded analysis! My goal was to
sweep you off your feet, Pip. And I can see that I
failed."

She gave a little, nervous laugh. "Wait a minute!
I'm not the one who's supposed to get swept off her
feet. Mary is. I just went along on this date as an
adviser, remember? My job was to give you feed-
back on how you were doing. You *did* say you
wanted constructive criticism," she reminded
him.

"Yes, but—"

"Good grief, Jeremy! I hope you weren't expecting me to fall *totally* into the romantic mood! After all, we both knew you were just practicing a lot of lines and flirtatious gambits to use on Mary. I'd have looked like a pretty big fool if I'd started taking it all to heart, now wouldn't I?"

She laughed again, but it sounded hollow. Unfortunately, that was just how big a fool she was, she acknowledged to herself. She *had* taken it all to heart.

There was a short silence. Jeremy appeared to be deep in troubled thought if the gloomy scowl that marred his brow was anything to go by. "It seems I've been guilty of overconfidence," he said finally. "You see, I went ahead and arranged to take Mary out tonight. I assumed I'd be ready, after our practice session last night. But now you've shown me that I'm not ready after all."

"But you *are!*" Pippi cried, dismayed at what her thoughtless words had done. "Forget my quibbling concerns—they don't matter. Let Mary experience the same evening you shared with me, and I can just about guarantee she'll fall in love with you!" And then it would be out of Pippi's hands and she could crawl away to lick her wounds in private.

"I'm not so sure of that," Jeremy said glumly. "I'd feel a lot better if I knew I had a back-up plan. That way, even if tonight doesn't do the trick, I'll be ready with Plan B. Help me come up with something, Pip?"

"Well . . . uh . . ." she muttered, floundering.

"You had a whole list of ideas, remember?"

"Mmm." She feverishly attempted to recall what had been on that list. But she had her doubts that any contingency plan was really necessary. It was impossible to imagine any normal woman failing to respond to the romantic wooing Jeremy had shown himself capable of. And if *that* wasn't effective, what chance was there that *any* plan would succeed?"

"I seem to recollect that your list contained a cryptic mention of 'athletic prowess,' " he said musingly. "I didn't ask at the time what you meant by that, since I wasn't sure I wanted to know, but maybe it's an idea we could use now."

What had she meant by "athletic prowess?" And then Pippi remembered what her reasoning had been when she included it on the list. Mary probably saw Jeremy as just a stuffy, sober-minded accountant, so what he needed to do was show her the more dashing, virile side of himself. And what better way than by demonstrating his athletic skill?

"Has Mary ever seen you play racquetball?" she asked.

"Sure. In fact, we've played together a few times."

"Oh. Then that's no good," she muttered in disappointment. "And if the sight of that gorgeous physique of yours in action didn't arouse her interest, you've got your work cut out for you! We'd better come up with a real daredevil sport, one that will knock her socks off."

He quirked a brow in amusement. "Did I just hear you say you think my physique is gorgeous?"

"I'm not blind, Jeremy. Of course I think it's gorgeous!" she said with brusque impatience, hoping to disguise her embarrassment. "But the point is, you apparently need a sport with a bit more drama and glamor than racquetball to impress this woman. What do you suggest?"

"Well, the snow's already melted, so it's too late for me to dazzle her on skis. And it's way too early in the year for any water sports. I don't drive race cars or ride horses or wrestle alligators. So I guess that leaves just one thing I'm good at that might be considered daredevil or dramatic. Unless you count my skill at Scrabble?" he added hopefully.

Pippi chuckled. "Watching you play Scrabble might turn *me* on, but I think Mary is a tougher nut to crack. So, what's this daring sport you're so good at?"

"Would you really get turned on watching me play Scrabble?" he asked curiously, and she groaned.

"What's with this insatiable ego of yours?" she demanded. "I was just making a joke, for crying out loud! Now, are you going to tell me how you plan to get Mary's attention or not?"

"Not," he said with a teasing grin. "You'll find out tomorrow."

"Why not now?"

"Because I'd rather *show* you than tell you, and I want it to be a surprise. That way, you can give me some idea of how Mary's likely to react."

"So I'm supposed to be your guinea pig again."

"If you want to call it that. Frankly, you're lots better looking than any guinea pig I ever saw. There's really no resemblance whatsoever," he said soothingly, and then shot her a wicked glance. "Except, of course, for the way you twitch that cute little nose of yours when you're confused."

"Why, Jeremy!" she exclaimed coyly, prepared to give him a taste of his own medicine. "I never knew you thought my nose was cute!"

"I've always adored your nose, Pip," he said softly, and for an instant there was more than teasing in his gaze. But then he leaned back in his chair and stretched. "I'll pick you up tomorrow morning at ten o'clock. Wear warm clothes."

"Now, just a minute! Maybe I'd rather sleep late and read the Sunday paper in bed tomorrow!" But

she wasn't protesting as loudly as she should have
been, because she was too busy trying not to burst
a blood vessel over the sight of his broad shoulders
and rounded biceps rippling and flexing beneath
his plaid shirt. "Where do you plan on going for
this athletic exhibition of yours?" she asked in
resignation.

But he wouldn't say. And even when Pippi
pointed out that the morning after his big night
with Mary was no time to be getting up early, he
just smiled and shook his head.

"Be ready at ten," he repeated firmly.

"Oh, I'll be ready," she assured him. "Ready to
get a phone call from you, telling me that your date
with Mary went so well there's no need to use Plan
B after all. Maybe you'll even be spending tomorrow
morning with her." She was shocked by the jagged
edge of pain that sawed through her chest at the
thought.

Jeremy actually blushed. "That won't happen,"
he said, looking down at the floor.

"We'll see."

There was no phone call. Sunday morning was
bright as a newly minted penny, but Pippi was in
no mood to enjoy it. All the previous night her
thoughts had kept returning to Jeremy and Mary,
wondering what intimate, romantic moment of his
night to remember they were sharing right then.

It got worse when she knew they would be dancing. Her head throbbed with the effort of trying not
to think about the other woman wrapped in the
magic circle of Jeremy's arms. And the pain was so
sharp when she imagined their good-night kiss
and what might follow that Pippi had put on her
coat and gone outside for a walk in the dark. The
possibility of encountering muggers or rapists had

seemed less threatening than her own thoughts just then.

She hadn't gotten much sleep, so the sound of Jeremy's cheerful whistling as he dashed up the last flight of stairs to her apartment made her grit her teeth.

"You sound mighty pleased about something," she said dourly as she opened the door to his beaming smile. "Your date with Mary must have been a big success."

Immediately, his face drooped into lines of despondency. "I'd rather not talk about it," he said. "Let's just concentrate on Plan B. It's a perfect day for it."

"But what happened?" Pippi felt she *had* to know, no matter how reluctant Jeremy was to discuss it!

"Nothing," he said baldly. "She was friendly, she was polite, she said she had a good time, but . . . nothing happened."

"Give her time," Pippi said reassuringly, ashamed of the way her heart suddenly felt so much lighter. Some friend *she* was, feeling glad when things went wrong for Jeremy! She would just have to try to make it up to him today, she vowed silently. Whatever he wanted her to do in her role as guinea pig for Plan B, she would do it.

Famous last words. Luckily for her own peace of mind, Pippi had no inkling of the challenge she was soon to face.

It wasn't long before they were out of town, driving along a narrow country road with freshly plowed fields and gently rolling green hills on either side. The sprightly notes of Bach's Brandenburg Concerto No. 3 cascaded from Jeremy's tape deck and rushed out the open windows on the light spring breeze.

Everywhere Pippi looked this sunny May morning, the countryside was clothing itself in festive new greenery and shimmering veils of pastel-tinted blossoms, ready to celebrate the glorious renaissance of life after the long, cold winter. The whole world shone fresh and new in the bright, sparkling air.

"Just look at those cumulus clouds!" Jeremy exclaimed gleefully, glancing up at the serene blue sky where flat-bottomed, fluffy white clouds moved like grazing sheep across an endless pasture.

Clouds? Pippi thought. On a day when the whole earth was decked out like a flower garden, he wanted to look at *clouds*? There was no accounting for tastes, she concluded. She herself preferred to look at the spring wildflowers blooming along the roadside.

She sneaked another look at Jeremy, and promptly forgot about looking at flowers. His face was glowing with the same vitality and fresh expectancy as the spring morning. His lithe, muscular body exuded life and strength and joy. She ached to touch him, to mold herself against his body and feel the powerful rhythmic beating of his heart echo in her own veins and stir her own blood in unison with his.

But instead she bit her lip and turned to stare blindly out the window. This kind of nonsense has got to stop, she told herself firmly.

"We're just about there," Jeremy said, and Pippi was intrigued by the undertone of suppressed excitement in his voice. Moments later he turned onto a dirt road that led toward a distant cluster of low buildings.

As they drew closer she began to make out one detail after another of the scene that lay before them. And what she saw made her heart leap into her throat with a suffocating feeling of dread.

There were about a dozen cars, some with long narrow trailers still attached, parked on the mown grass in front of a large, aluminum-sided building with a wide, gaping doorway. It looked ominously like an airplane hangar. There were people—some scurrying about in energetic activity, some standing still and gazing skyward with binoculars, and some just sitting in lawn chairs drawn up along a wide, grassy track. It looked like a runway, but Pippi hoped desperately that it was not.

But finally, there were several odd-looking small aircraft lolling at awkward angles so that one long, slender wing rested on the ground and the other pointed upward. To Pippi's horrified eyes, they resembled nothing so much as large dead birds with grotesquely stiffened wings, toppled askew in rigor mortis.

She pressed her fist against her mouth and tried to stay calm. There was nothing to be afraid of. The images of death and destruction were all in her head, and they were part of a problem she'd been trying to lick for years and years—her fear of heights.

"So, how do you like *this* surprise?" Jeremy asked triumphantly. Fortunately, he didn't wait for a reply. He was too busy waving at people. They all seemed glad to see him and called out jovial greetings as he got out of the car. Feeling numb with terror, Pippi got out too.

"What is this place?" she managed to ask.

"It's the center for the soaring club I belong to." Somebody called his name and Jeremy's face split in a wide grin as he strode across the makeshift parking lot toward the man. "Looks like everybody's out here today, and no wonder! The weather conditions are damn near perfect," he said over his shoulder to Pippi, who trailed along at his heels.

He introduced her to a handful of people, but their names went in one ear and out the other. Their conversation was full of terms she didn't understand, but she was scarcely listening. She was too busy hoping that Jeremy didn't have anything more challenging planned for her than to stay on the ground and watch. Even that would be an ordeal. Flying was a subject she had always preferred not even to think about, hear about, or read about, much less *see.*

When Jeremy turned to her a few minutes later, his eyes were so full of boyish delight that she got the feeling he couldn't see past it to *her*, even when he looked straight into her white, drawn face.

"Why don't you wait here while we bring out my sailplane?" he suggested. "Just don't get in the way of the tow plane when it lands."

She gulped and nodded.

"Our turn should come in about half an hour," he continued. "So be patient." He gave her an ecstatic smile. "You and I will be heading up into the wild blue yonder before you know it!" He turned and headed for the hangar.

Pippi gave a strangled moan and shut her eyes. It took every ounce of her strength and determination to keep on standing instead of slumping to the ground in a quivering, jellylike mass. But she had promised herself she would go through with this no matter what.

"You can do it," she whispered. After all, she *had* flown before. But that had been in a DC-10, and she'd been so doped up with tranquilizers, she'd managed to convince herself that the huge jet was just a rather large bus. Except for some bad moments during takeoff and landing, she'd been quite successful at pretending the "bus" was safely on the ground for the whole trip!

Little planes were something else again. She glanced quickly at the waiting aircraft and then looked away, shuddering. How could you pretend you were on the ground if you were tossing around over nothingness in a flimsy little thing like that? It looked about as sturdy as an egg carton.

Time passed. Pippi stayed right where she was. When she heard the drone of an airplane engine, she glanced up to make sure she wasn't in its path. She wasn't. The sight of the little plane bobbing toward the ground, bucking as its wheels touched down, made her feel dizzy and sick. After that she refused to look up when planes landed and took off. She didn't want to see.

She did force herself to watch Jeremy and his friends push his plane out onto the grassy runway and position it so its nose pointed directly into the wind. Jeremy fussed over it like a mother hen over a baby chick, giving it a final preflight check. That should have been reassuring, but Pippi couldn't help feeling like a condemned prisoner watching the hangman inspect the gallows.

"How much do you weigh, Pip?" Jeremy asked, consulting his clipboard papers. He chuckled at her answer. "This'll be almost like carrying no passenger at all."

If only! she thought.

The dreaded moment came at last. Jeremy helped her up the side of the plane and down into the open cockpit—there was no door. The plane jounced and rocked beneath her, and she was reminded of boarding a ride at an amusement park. Only this was a thousand times more terrifying.

Jeremy strapped her into the passenger seat

directly behind the pilot's seat, and she gripped the sides of the plane in white-knuckled fear. Then he took his place and reached back to close the clear plastic canopy over the cockpit.

Pippi squeezed her eyes tightly shut and concentrated on trying to control her ragged, shallow breathing. She was taken completely by surprise when the plane suddenly began to move. How could that be, when Jeremy hadn't even started the engine yet? Her eyes flew open in panic. "Omigosh!" she whispered.

Their wheels were drumming over the uneven ground and a man was running alongside, holding the wing level. Up ahead, another plane was also gathering speed on the runway, and a long rope stretched taut between the two aircraft.

"Jeremy, what's—"

"I can't talk right now," he cut her off tersely, concentrating on working the controls to keep his sailplane in position as it rose silently off the ground. Soon the heavier tow plane ahead of them was also in the air, and it banked slowly to the left and started climbing, pulling them upward.

Pippi felt the last dregs of strength in her clenched muscles dissolve into an icy vapor of fear. She knew, though she refused to look, that the ground was dropping away beneath them at a merciless pace. Its safety was irretrievably lost to her. Why, why, *why* were they doing this? If Jeremy's plane was so cockeyed that somebody had to hold the wing steady and it needed a tow to get into the air, why would anyone risk flying it?

"What was it you wanted to ask me?" he inquired after several minutes, still keeping his gaze on the instrument panel.

Her mouth felt so dry she could scarcely speak. "Wh-why is that plane towing us?"

His head swiveled around and he gave her a startled glance. "It's towing us so we can get to a good altitude for soaring, of course," he said. His eyes flicked back to the array of gauges at the front of the cockpit. "And my altimeter tells me we're just about there. Twenty-one hundred feet." He reached forward and pulled a small red knob. There was a loud metallic *ping*, followed by an eerie silence.

"What happened?" Pippi gasped as they dipped and banked sharply to the right. A dizzying sweep of distant landscape rolled before her, a crazy-quilt patchwork of brown and green fields. She gave a groan of terror and snapped her gaze away, desperately searching the sky for the other plane. She spotted it turning left and descending away from them, pulling the slack, empty towline after it. There was no sound but the quiet swishing of the wind.

"I just released the towline," Jeremy said.

"But you forgot to turn the motor on! We're falling!" she shrieked.

"Don't be crazy, Pip! A glider doesn't *have* a motor. And we are *not* falling."

"A glider?" Had she missed something? Just then they hit a small pocket of turbulence, and the sailplane bucked like a rubber raft on whitewater rapids. "Omigosh!" She moaned. "We're gonna die!"

"Pip, be reasonable," Jeremy pleaded in exasperation.

"But there's nothing holding us up here!" she said, her breath catching in sobs as she stared out at the limpid blue emptiness surrounding them. She refused to look down for fear of seeing the ground rushing up at her like a killer tidal wave.

"Nonsense," he said calmly. "The upward angle

of the front edge of the wing against the oncoming air current creates high pressure underneath the wing, forcing it upward. And the corresponding low pressure on top of the wing creates a vacuum which—"

"Aughh!" she shrieked. "How can you give me a physics lecture at a time like this? Can't you see I'm about to have a nervous breakdown?"

He turned around in his seat and fixed her with a concerned gaze, this time really *seeing* her. "Omigosh!" He echoed Pippi's perennial exclamation of dismay. "You're really frightened, aren't you?"

"I'm scared out of my wits! Jeremy, shouldn't you be watching the sky in front of us or something? When you turn around like that, it makes me feel so . . ."

He faced forward again, but his attention was still on her. "Pip, I guarantee there's no danger. I'm a trained glider pilot with hours and hours of soaring experience. We're safer up here than we would be driving a car on the highway." His deep voice resonated with calm, reassuring certainty. "Don't you know I would never take risks with something as precious as your life?"

"But the ground is so far away," she protested, relaxing a little in spite of herself in response to his soothing words and tone.

"There's nothing to be afraid of. Just look at that hawk up above us and to the right, circling on the updraft. Tell me—does he look worried?"

"No, but he's a bird and we're not!"

"Ah, but sometimes, on a day like today, we can come close," he said huskily. "Relax, Pip, and let me show you how it feels."

When he used that rich, enticing voice on her, she would promise him anything. She remained silent as they headed for a spot directly below where the hawk was still soaring effortlessly on outstretched wings. And then she felt an odd, queasy sensation in the pit of her stomach, as if she'd just stepped onto an elevator that was speeding toward the penthouse suite of a skyscraper.

"What's happening to us?" she asked fearfully.

"We've just entered a mass of warm, rising air and it's taking us upward. We're soaring exactly like that hawk you saw. Doesn't it feel great?"

Truthfully, she wasn't sure. She felt as fragile and unprotected as a feather being tossed on the breeze as Jeremy banked the sailplane in a series of turns that kept them rising in a seemingly endless, dizzying spiral.

Something in her silence must have communicated to him that she wasn't necessarily enjoying this. "Put your trust in me, Pip," he urged in a strong, compelling voice that gentled her as it persuaded her. "Let yourself go. Taste the freedom of soaring swift and silent as a bird. Tell your fear to rest its fluttering wings, because Mother Nature is holding you in the very palm of her hand. And so am I."

"Mmm," she sighed appreciatively. "That's pretty poetic stuff for an accountant." She let his words work their magic, weaving a spell of safety over her. She was in Jeremy's hands and she knew instinctively that he would never let her fall.

The panic in her ebbed, leaving a feeling of buoyancy and weightlessness. Suddenly fearless, she felt at one with the universe as she and Jeremy dipped and glided and soared over invisible peaks and valleys of air, all drenched in the bright gold and blue of sunlight and sky.

"It's like dancing," she said breathlessly. "Except you can't hear the music—only *feel* it."

Jeremy turned his head and his eyes met hers in a glowing look that was like a visual embrace. What passed between them in that moment transcended normal human communication. Never before had Pippi felt this sense of something so intensely shared.

The rest of the flight passed in a shimmering haze of brilliant sensation as they gradually lost altitude, gliding down through the air like a sled sliding down a snowy slope. Even when they were landing, Pippi felt scarcely a twinge of nervousness as she saw the hard ground whizzing by beneath them just before they lightly touched down.

Her legs were weak and trembly as Jeremy lifted her out of the sailplane and down to solid earth. He held her as if she were priceless crystal of infinite fragility. How she yearned to nestle her head against his chest and stay within his sheltering arms. They belonged together, she and Jeremy, after what they'd just shared.

The thought stopped her cold. How could they belong together when he was in love with another woman? Pippi was only a guinea pig on this flight. And whatever magic Jeremy had shown her today, he would share with Mary one day soon.

She felt numb as she drew back from the tender clasp of his hands. Once again, it seemed she had managed to fall in love with the wrong man.

Six

"How about lunch?" Jeremy suggested a half hour later as they were heading back toward Minneapolis. "Or are you still too shook up to eat?"

"I'm fine now," Pippi said firmly. "You've already fussed over me enough, Jeremy."

He gave her a quick, assessing glance. "Yup, you've got the roses back in your cheeks finally. So we can go ahead with my original plans."

"What plans?"

"For a picnic lunch." He turned down a rough, rutted road that gave the shock absorbers on his car a grueling workout. A few minutes later he pulled off the road and took a cooler and an old blanket out of the back.

"Do you feel up to walking as far as that patch of sun you can see just through those trees?" he asked solicitously.

"There's nothing wrong with my legs. Of course I can walk that far."

"Good. If you change your mind, just let me know, and I'll carry you the rest of the way."

Her legs turned wobbly at the mere thought. The last thing she needed right now was to wind up in Jeremy's arms again!

The "patch of sun" turned out to be a charming woodland glade carpeted with grass and flowers. A gurgling brook and the chattering of nesting birds filled the clearing with pleasant sounds.

"Mmm, it's nice here," Pippi said, lying back against the blanket with her arms stretched over her head, feeling the sun's warmth on her face.

"Don't get too relaxed," Jeremy warned as he unloaded the cooler. "You've got some explaining to do."

Her body went stiff and her right hand clenched a clump of grass growing at the edge of the blanket. She sat up slowly, looking him directly in the eye as she tried to bluff her way out of it. "What do you mean?"

"Don't I have a right to know why you've been keeping this a secret from me all these months?" he asked with an encouraging smile as he handed her a thick corned beef sandwich and an ice-cold bottle of beer from the cooler.

"What secret?" Had he guessed so quickly her guilty love for him? Was that why his eyes were full of sympathy? But what did he mean by "all these months?" She hadn't been loving him that long . . . had she?

"Be honest, Pip. You've got a deep-rooted fear of flying. And I refuse to believe that today was the first time you've realized that! What were you thinking of, to let me take you up there without telling me?"

She breathed a mental sigh of relief. So that's what he meant by her "secret." She hastened to set him straight on the exact nature of her phobia. "It's not exactly fear of flying—"

"Don't give me thàt! I've never seen anyone as terrified as you were today! For a while there I was afraid you were going to rip off your safety harness and jump over the side without a parachute!"

"I'm not that crazy. But I will confess to an irrational fear of heights. It comes and goes, but I've been battling it since I was a little girl, and I hate to give in to it. That's why I didn't tell you. I was hoping I could control my fears on my own this time."

"But don't you realize what a risk you took? What if you'd come completely unglued up there? Panic is too damned dangerous and unpredictable to play games with in a sailplane at two thousand feet!"

"I'm sorry. I thought I could handle it," she said faintly.

"And, as usual, you were determined to conquer it all on your own, without asking for help from anyone!" he concluded in exasperation. "Can't you see that stubborn independence isn't the answer to every problem, Pip?"

"You're right." She sighed. "I don't know what I would have done up there today without you to give me the reassurance I needed. Because of you I ended up having a wonderful time. I'm sure Mary will love it too," she added quickly.

"Don't try to change the subject! We're talking about *you*, Pip. I want to hear more about this fear you say you've had all your life. How did it start?"

"I fell off the roof when I was nine years old."

"You *what*?"

"I fell off the roof," she repeated, smiling at his look of shock. "And I wound up in the hospital with a concussion, a broken arm, a broken collarbone, and more bruises than I care to remember. Plus a few emotional problems when it came to getting more than six feet off the ground."

"But what the hell were you doing on the roof in the first place?"

"Um . . ." She took a bite of her sandwich to stall for time, and discovered that Jeremy had been rather heavy-handed with his favorite hot spicy mustard. Her eyes watered, and she quickly gulped down a swig of beer.

"Pippi!" Jeremy protested at her delaying tactics.

"Promise you won't laugh?"

"Do I look like I'm in a laughing mood? Why would I laugh at something that put a nine-year-old girl in the hospital?"

"Because it is rather funny," she confessed. "You see, I climbed up on the roof and tried to run along the ridgepole to the chimney because I wanted to be just like Pippi Longstocking."

Jeremy didn't say a thing. He just stared at her as if he were waiting for her words to start making sense. Then he shook his head. "*Who* is Pippi Longstocking and what was *she* doing on the roof?"

Pippi tried to keep a straight face. "*She* was playing a game of tag with two policemen who wanted to put her into an orphanage."

"You're making this up!"

"No, I'm not. Pippi Longstocking is a character in a children's book by Astrid Lindgren. I was named after her because of my red hair, and for years and years she was my personal heroine. I suppose she still is in a way," she added thoughtfully.

"Even after her bad example landed you in the hospital?"

"Even after that," she admitted. "You see, Pippi

was so strong and brave and funny. And bad things couldn't hurt her. Burglars, bullies, policemen—she handled them all with such outrageous flair."

"She must have been quite a girl." His voice was suddenly soft, and his eyes, too, as he watched the memories of childhood flit across Pippi's face.

"Oh, she was! And she was strong enough to lift a horse."

"I hope you didn't try doing that too!"

"No. Luckily there were no horses in my neighborhood. But I did almost smother myself trying to sleep like Pippi, with my feet on the pillow and the covers over my head. And when I tried to imitate her 'morning exercises'—forty-three somersaults in a row—I got so dizzy I almost threw up!" She chuckled.

Jeremy frowned. "I hate to say this, Pip, but she doesn't sound like a very positive influence."

"Then I must be explaining it wrong. You see, she helped me feel braver, because I knew that *she* could stand up to the things that frightened me."

The urge to make Jeremy understand was so strong that Pippi plunged on, not stopping to consider how much of herself she might reveal to him. "When other kids poked fun at her, she didn't care. And even though her father wasn't—"

She stopped so suddenly that her mouth froze upon the words. What had made her mention *that*? It wasn't something she liked to talk about. Not ever.

"Her father wasn't what?" Jeremy asked very gently. His hand reached out to rest against her knee, offering unspoken, instinctive comfort.

"Nothing." She stared hard at the toe of her right sneaker.

"Trust me, Pip. If something's bothering you, you don't have to bear it all alone. I'll help."

"It's no big deal. Just . . . her father had disappeared. He wasn't around. But Pippi Longstocking never worried about it or felt bad. She was sure he'd come back someday."

A tear ran down her cheek and off her chin, then splashed on Jeremy's hand on her knee. She was furious with herself. What a weird, stupid thing to do, crying over a missing father in a children's book. Jeremy would think she was crazy as a loon.

"What about *your* father, Pip?" he whispered. "Did *you* worry and feel bad because of him?"

"Yes." The word was almost swallowed up by an anguished sob. "Because he went away and never came back."

Somewhere inside her a dam seemed to burst. Pippi felt for a moment that she must surely drown in the renewed tide of loss and grief that swept up from deep in her past to overwhelm her once again. But then Jeremy's strong arms closed around her in a circle of warmth and comfort. He gently removed the sandwich and beer bottle from her hands, then drew her close against his broad chest.

"Cry all you need to, Pip," he murmured against her ear, stroking her soft, windblown curls. "I'll be here to hold you. And I'm a good listener. You already know that."

She managed a choked snuffle of laughter. "Because all I ever do is tell you my troubles."

"But there are some troubles you've never told me." He handed her his handkerchief, and while Pippi wiped her eyes his words hung in the air, both a question and an invitation.

She nodded and took a deep breath. "My father

left us when I was four. You wouldn't think I was old enough to remember him, really, but I was."

"What do you remember?" Jeremy's hand stroked up and down her back.

"Sometimes he'd come sit by my bed late at night and tell me about the party he'd just been to. He always smelled of cologne and cigarettes and whiskey and chewing gum. His clothes were different from what other fathers on our block wore. Brighter, fancier. And he had a smile that would make you do almost anything to please him, just so he'd smile at you."

She paused, wondering what Jeremy was thinking. But all he said was, "Go on."

"He and Mom used to fight. I felt so frightened, listening to them. Arri and Char were frightened, too, I think, but they wouldn't talk about it."

The worst part lay just ahead, and Pippi shivered in Jeremy's arms. "Once I woke up in the middle of the night and heard Mom crying. I knew it was because of *him*, and that made me mad. So when he came into my room and tried to talk to me, I turned my face away and pretended to be asleep." She drew a deep, shuddering breath. "That was the night he left for good. I never saw him again."

"And you've blamed yourself ever since." Jeremy's quiet voice held no uncertainty. Somehow he knew.

"Yes." She looked him full in the face and was deeply touched by the compassionate understanding in his warm eyes. She sighed. "For years I would've given anything to have a second chance. A chance to show my father how much I really loved him, in spite of everything." She laughed ruefully. "As if knowing that, he would have stayed."

"I doubt it." Jeremy's voice was very gentle.

"So do I. My grown-up self can plainly see that his leaving had nothing to do with me. The trouble was between him and my mother. But there's still a little girl somewhere inside me who feels terribly sure it was all her fault."

"Tell that little girl she's wrong. Tell her *I* said so!" Jeremy said gruffly. "And if she gives you any argument, tell her I'll hug her until all those bad feelings get squeezed right out of her."

He clasped her hard against his body in vivid demonstration. It felt so good that Pippi found herself believing that if only she could stay in Jeremy's arms long enough, all the pain of her father's long-ago desertion might indeed be squeezed away. But she'd never know for sure, because staying in Jeremy's arms was the one thing she must *not* do!

She backed out of his hug and tried to laugh. "That glider ride must have shaken me up more than I realized. It certainly jarred my tongue loose. I've been talking a lot of emotional drivel. How did we get on such a gloomy topic anyway?"

Jeremy's eyes darkened with hurt and anger, but he spoke so quietly that Pippi could hear the bees buzzing in the nearby flowers. "I realize that you're embarrassed because you let me get so close just now," he said. "But that doesn't give you the right to kick me in the teeth when you push me away again."

"But I didn't—"

"It meant a lot to me that you would share such private, poignant memories with me, Pip. Don't spoil it now by calling them drivel."

He was right. Fear had made her cruel. She'd been scared to death that his comfort and understanding might tempt her into betraying her feelings for him, so she had tried to destroy the moment of caring and intimacy they'd shared. And Jeremy deserved better than that.

"I'm sorry," she whispered. "Talking about my father, after all these years, was pretty heavy. I guess I'm not handling it very well. But I do appreciate the shoulder to cry on."

"Anytime you need it, it's all yours." His crooked smile seemed to reach right out and carve a jagged line across her heart.

"Mary might have something to say about *that*," she said. "After all, she's got a prior claim on that shoulder of yours."

"But your claim will always be good, Pip," he said softly, flushing slightly as he turned away to rummage in the ice chest. "How about another beer? The one you've got must be warm by now. And I won't be hurt if you scrape some of that mustard off your sandwich," he added, noting the cautious way she was eyeing it before taking another bite.

She smiled at him gratefully and scraped off the mustard. A warm, companionable silence enfolded them as they ate their picnic lunch and let their bodies soak up the spring sunshine.

Nibbling the last cookie a half hour later, Pippi began to feel drowsy. The past few hours had been emotionally draining. And she hadn't gotten much sleep the night before.

"I'd better get you home, sleepyhead," Jeremy said, gathering up the picnic things. "You stay put while I load this stuff in the car, and I'll be back for you in just a minute."

Pippi knew she ought to stand up and start walking after him. But she felt so comfortable all stretched out on the sunwarmed blanket and it was so hard to keep her eyes open. She would get up in just a minute though. Of course she would.

She woke up in Jeremy's arms as he carried her to the car. "Put me down," she protested sleepily, even as her arms curled around his neck.

He smiled and shook his head. "You've had a tough day, Pip. This is the least I can do after dragging you up into the air in my sailplane and making you relive the trauma of falling off a roof."

"I didn't mind. Not after you made me feel safe."

He scarcely heard her. Pippi was so light and fragile in his arms that he felt a sharp physical pain at the thought of her small body hurtling to the ground all those years ago.

Shifting her weight onto just his left arm, he reached up with his right hand and traced the length of her arm from the fine bones of her wrist to the firm curve of her shoulder. "Where did it break?" he asked huskily.

Pippi gave a nervous little laugh. "Actually, it was the other arm." She pointed out the site of the fracture, then shivered as Jeremy caressed the flesh over the place where the broken bone had knit back together.

Next, his fingers dipped beneath the collar of her shirt and ran along the delicate line of her collarbone. "The right side or the left?" he asked.

"The right." She felt the gentle pressure of his fingers pause there, spreading warmth over her skin.

"And a concussion too?"

She nodded. She didn't understand the pain and helpless anger in his brown eyes as he tenderly cupped her head with the palm of his hand, feeling the contours of her skull beneath her bright hair.

"It wasn't really so bad," she tried to reassure him. "And actually, something wonderful happened because I fell off that roof."

"I'll bet." His voice was gruff with disbelief.

"Really, it did. While I was in the hospital my doctor was Dr. Haugen, and he was kind and funny and had the *nicest* blue eyes. Before my bruises had faded, he and Mom fell in love. And that's how I got the best stepfather in the whole world!" she concluded triumphantly.

"By falling off a roof." Jeremy shook his head in exasperated wonderment. "Rather an extreme approach to matchmaking, Pip."

"I didn't do it on purpose! But Dad still likes to tease me by calling me his little red-headed cupid." She was struck by a sudden thought. "And now I'm playing cupid again, for you and Mary. I hope I don't have to fall off a roof to get you two together!"

"Don't you dare even go near a roof!" They were back at the car by now, and Jeremy punctuated his order by yanking open the car door and summarily depositing Pippi in the passenger seat.

"I promise." She sighed. The thought of Jeremy and Mary getting together at all was thoroughly depressing. What an impossible predicament she'd gotten herself into! Here she was, hopelessly in love with Jeremy, but pledged to help him win the heart of another woman. Talk about a conflict of interest!

And right now she was much too sleepy to come up with a solution to the problem. How *did* one go about falling out of love with someone like Jeremy? It sounded close to impossible. But she would figure out something . . . later. For now it was easier just to fall back to sleep.

Pippi dreamed she was flying. She was a bird with long white wings, lifting upward into the dazzling reaches of the sky. But even in flight she was warm and safe, because she was in Jeremy's hands. It felt wonderful.

"Pip, wake up," Jeremy's voice said softly. "I can't find your keys. Wake up, love."

Her eyes flew open in confusion. "What?"

"Where'd you put your keys? I need them to unlock your door." He was standing on her front doorstep, balancing her barely awake body against him with one arm while with his free hand he clumsily searched through her purse.

It was hard to come down out of the clouds for something as mundane as a set of keys. Pippi wrinkled her brow and twitched her nose as she tried to remember what she'd done with them.

"I think . . . my jacket pocket."

Jeremy checked her pockets and shook his head.

"My jeans?" she suggested next.

The flat of Jeremy's palm slid down her rounded denim-clad curves, feeling for the bulge of her keys. Just the casual touch of his fingers on her buttocks made Pippi tingle with sensual awareness.

When that search proved futile, his hands moved to the front pockets of her jeans. With his face carefully averted and a tinge of color staining his cheekbones, he gingerly reached inside her right pocket.

Pippi felt a floodtide of sexual longing crest within her as his fingers brushed over her hipbone and down toward the intimate hollows of her womanhood. The cotton lining of her jeans pocket was no barrier to the current of desire generated by his touch.

The keys weren't there.

Jeremy groaned with frustration and reached blindly for the left pocket. His trembling hand slid between the layers of fabric that imprisoned the warmth of her body. Perspiration beaded his forehead as his fingers descended over the faint ridge that marked the top of her panties. And then he felt the hard edge of a key.

He released his breath in a pent-up sigh and drew the keys from her pocket. Pippi relaxed her tense, tautened muscles. If the search had gone on for ten seconds more, she couldn't have answered for her sanity.

Jeremy unlocked the door and strode up the stairs as if the hounds of hell were after him. Pippi clung to his shoulders for dear life. When he stopped to unlock the door to her apartment, she decided it was time to point out the obvious.

"I'm awake now, Jeremy. You don't have to carry me anymore." Her voice was breathless, as if she herself had just run up all those stairs.

"Oh." He looked down at her in a sort of dazed surprise. "That's true." The fierce grip of his fingers and the taut pressure of his arms eased their hold on her. His hands supported her at the waist, as slowly she slid down the length of his body until her feet touched the floor.

She felt the warm, flexed knotting of his thigh muscles. She felt her own heart pounding against her ribs just above where his hands spanned her waist. The moment was charged with powerful yearning and unspeakable tension. Did Jeremy feel it too?

"Thanks for taking me soaring," she said huskily. "It was unforgettable."

"Sure. Just like falling off a roof, right?" His smile mixed the tender with the wry. Oh, that smile! Pippi wanted to lift her hand to the shy curve of his lips and take their imprint away with her, safely cupped in the palm of her hand.

"It was *nothing* like falling off a roof," she assured him. "And I oughta know!"

Which one of them would be the first to step

away and break the lingering contact of their bodies? she wondered. Didn't he notice that she was still so close she could feel his every breath as if it were her own.

"Pip?" The hesitant, questioning murmur made her heart go still. "If—"

It sounded like such a promising start. *If.* So fraught with possibilities! "Yes?"

He looked awkward and unsure. He flicked her key ring with a finger, setting it jingling where it hung from the lock on her door. He took a deep breath. Finally, the anxious question spilled out of him.

"If you were Mary, do you think you might have fallen in love with me today?"

Pippi took a giant step backward. Right away she made a decision to keep smiling. No matter what. No matter if her lips felt like defective rubber bands. No matter if her chest felt as if she'd just instantly contracted bronchial pneumonia. No matter if she wanted to push Jeremy down the stairs. She'd keep smiling.

"Pip, what I meant to say was—"

She was smiling so hard she didn't even hear him. She smiled as she drew her key out of the lock, opened the door, and stepped inside. She smiled as she turned to deliver her parting words, in answer to his original question.

"You never know. Some women will fall for anything."

Seven

Twenty minutes later Pippi was no longer smiling. She was down on her hands and knees, furiously scrubbing her kitchen floor.

But it was such a small kitchen—hardly more than a cubicle—that she'd had to scrub the floor three times to get any satisfaction out of it. Maybe it was time to start in on the bathroom. Anything to take her mind off Jeremy.

When the phone rang, she peeled off her rubber gloves and hurried out to the living room, wafting a strong odor of pine-scented ammonia in her wake.

"Hello?" She was slightly out of breath from wielding the scrub brush so fiercely.

"Don't tell me I caught you in the shower *again*!" her sister Charlotte exclaimed.

"No, Char." Pippi smiled in spite of herself. "What makes you think you did?"

"Because you're using that tone of voice you always use when you're dripping with soapy water."

Pippi held the phone away from her ear and eyed it with a puzzled frown. How could Char possibly guess such a thing? Here she was, spattered with soapy water, her jeans soaking from kneeling on the wet floor, and her big sister claimed to know it all just from the sound of her voice!

"Actually, you caught me scrubbing the kitchen floor," she admitted.

The silence on the other end of the line was deafening.

"You were *what*?" Char asked at last, her voice squeaking with incredulity.

"Scrubbing. The kitchen floor."

"I see." There was a long, long pause. "Pippi, I want you to sit down. Never mind getting the furniture wet, just sit. Take a deep breath. Now. Tell me what's wrong."

Pippi tightened her jaw and blinked back tears. She didn't feel ready to talk about Jeremy just yet. It was all too new and raw and painful. And confusing.

"Pippi, honey, I know something's bothering you. Arri called me yesterday, and according to her, you sounded sort of upset last week. And now *this*!"

"Now *what*?"

"Scrubbing floors. You never scrub floors without provocation."

"I *was* provoked! That floor had waxy build-up." Her voice suddenly broke. "Oh, Char. What am I going to do?"

"Just tell me the whole story. It's probably not half as bad as you think it is," her sister said soothingly.

"Wanna bet?" Pippi smiled grimly. "Char, I'm in love."

A horrified gasp was Char's first response. "Oh, Pippi, *no*! Not again! Not so soon!"

"I'm afraid so."

"But you only just got untangled from the last creep you thought you were in love with!"

"Arri told you all about my breakup with Marc, I suppose." Pippi sighed. Even though she and her sisters lived hundreds of miles apart from one another, the Smith family grapevine was awesomely efficient.

"Of course she told me. It was the best news I'd heard all week! So why do you want to spoil everything by rushing headlong into another disaster?"

"I d-don't *want* to." Pippi sniffled tearfully. "But it's too late. I already h-*have*."

"Damn. Who is it this time?"

"J-Jeremy."

"Jeremy? You mean, *your friend Jeremy*?"

"Uh-huh."

"Your friend Jeremy with the cute brown eyes and the great sense of humor and the rippling biceps?" The incredulous delight and approval in Char's voice made Pippi feel even more wretched.

"Yeah, that's the one. My friend Jeremy . . . who's passionately in love with another woman."

That brought the conversation to a screeching halt for several seconds.

Finally, Char recovered enough to say, "Oh, Pippi, I'm sorry. What are you going to do?"

"I was hoping you'd tell *me*. Isn't that what big sisters are for?" She paused, then asked in desperation, "How do I fall out of love with him, Char?"

"Are you sure there's no chance of getting him to fall in love with *you*, instead?"

"No chance." She left it at that. Explaining the whole screwy situation would take too much time.

"What a waste. Here you've finally fallen for a guy

who might actually make you happy, and it turns out he's not available!" Char sighed gustily. "Damn. I thought that only happened to me."

"Char! You mean *you* . . ."

"Last time I met a man I liked who wasn't married, he was engaged to be married in three days! So you've come to the right place for advice on how to talk yourself out of wanting a man you can't have. I'm an expert at it."

"Does your method always work?" Pippi asked hesitantly. She suddenly felt more concerned for Char than she was for herself.

"So far, yes."

·Pippi breathed a secret sigh of relief for Char's sake, and for her own.

"But it hasn't always been easy," her sister warned. "First, you've got to wrap yourself up in other things. Especially your work. In your case, you should try to eat and breathe and sleep photography for a while. And then try whatever else you can think of to take your mind off him—sports, politics, stamp collecting, you name it."

"Scrubbing floors?" Pippi suggested wryly.

"If it helps, sure. And make some new friends. Meet new people. New *men*." Char stopped to catch her breath. "Are you getting all this?"

"Yes, and I'm grateful, but . . ." She hesitated. There was no tactful way to tell Char that she was prescribing Band-Aids when what the patient really needed was open heart surgery.

But Char, in typical big-sisterly fashion, seemed to read her mind. "I don't know any miracle cures, Pippi. I'm just telling you what works for me." She paused, as if debating the wisdom of what she was about to say. "Of course, if you're really desperate, you could always . . ."

"Tell me!" Pippi pleaded. "I'll try anything!"

"All right. It might help if you spent some time with both of them together—Jeremy and this other woman." Pippi gave a muffled gasp of protest, but Char hurried on. "There's no quicker or more brutal way to convince yourself that you've got no place in a man's life. It'll hurt like hell, but it should do the trick."

"If you say so." Pippi gulped. "Come to think of it, I've never even met Mary. Maybe part of me still hasn't fully accepted the fact that she even *exists*. But once I meet her—"

"You'll know for sure that it's hopeless," Char completed the sentence for her.

"Now, *there's* something to look forward to!" But underneath the sarcasm Pippi had painfully resigned herself to following Char's suggestion. She thanked her sister for the advice and said good-bye, promising to let her know how it all turned out.

"You want me to *what*?" Jeremy demanded.

"Give a dinner party. I think it'll be a great way to impress Mary. She can see your house, meet your friends, and taste your cooking." Pippi forced a smile. "You'll have her hooked before you know it!"

She watched Jeremy shift uneasily on the old, sagging couch in the back room at her studio. He frowned down at the cup full of black coffee in his hand.

"I'm not sure that's a good idea," he said. "My cooking isn't all that impressive."

"Nonsense. How about those boneless chicken breasts with Gruyère cheese and brandy you fixed for me on my birthday?"

"That was different." He shot her a slightly harried, puzzled look. "Is this what your 'urgent' message on my answering machine was all about?

You wanted me to see you right away just so you could tell me to throw a *party*?"

"But I thought you'd be pleased that I've come up with a new plan for getting you and Mary together!" Pippi exclaimed.

"It's not what I expected," he said softly. "When I got your message, I thought you wanted to talk to me about . . . yesterday."

"What's to talk about?" Her chest tightened, but she shrugged.

"I got the feeling," he said carefully, "that you were upset by something I said when I brought you home. Whatever it was, I wish you'd tell me, Pip."

It wasn't easy to look directly into those earnest, concerned eyes and lie through her teeth, but Pippi did it. "There was nothing like that. I wasn't upset."

But Jeremy looked unconvinced.

"Forget about yesterday!" she insisted desperately. "What I want to know is, should I bring a salad or a dessert to your dinner party for Mary? And don't you think Friday night would be a good time to have it?"

Jeremy dropped his forehead against his clenched fist and shook his head helplessly. Finally, he chuckled wryly.

"Friday night it is. And yes, you and Marc *are* invited. And please bring a salad *and* a dessert."

You and Marc. Uh-oh. How was she going to get out of this one?

"Um, Marc might not be able to make it. I'll let you know." She twisted her fingers together in her lap. "Would you mind if I came alone, or do you prefer to have your guests neatly paired off like the animals on Noah's ark?"

"I prefer the pleasure of your company any way I can get it," he assured her, and Pippi felt her cheeks grow warm. How did one fall out of love with a man who said things like *that*?

"Then it's settled," she said briskly. "I'll see you Friday night."

"Not sooner? How about another planning session?"

"No. I'm going to be snowed under with work this week." She glanced at her watch. "That reminds me, my next sitting is in three minutes."

He lifted the cup of coffee in a farewell salute. "See you on Friday then. But don't be surprised if I call up asking for advice about this damn dinner party."

It wasn't hard to follow Char's suggestion to wrap herself up in her work. Pippi had a heavy schedule of portrait sittings to keep her busy during the day, and she'd been hired to photograph two large parties that week. What spare time she had, she spent in the darkroom, developing and printing some rolls of black and white film she'd shot two weeks earlier on a trip to the zoo with Jeremy.

As soon as she took a good look at her sheet of preliminary contact prints for the zoo trip, she realized this was *not* what Char had had in mind. Sure, there were plenty of good shots of children—a serious little girl eating an ice cream cone, a chunky-faced boy watching in delight as a monkey clambered up a rope, and a toddler sleeping soundly on his father's shoulder. But the most engagingly boyish face of all, the one that kept cropping up in frame after frame, was not that of a child. It was Jeremy's.

The eye of her camera had unerringly turned to him all that afternoon, like the eyes of a woman in love. His every mood, action, and reaction had been lovingly rendered on film. It was as if her camera had known, even before she herself had, that he was more to her than just a friend.

Obviously, the thing to do was to put this particular batch of film away and work on something else. That went without saying. Instead, Pippi went ahead and made enlarged prints of nearly every shot of Jeremy.

When they were all hung up to dry, she stared hungrily at his strong, warm, friendly face repeated in pose after pose. So much for her plan to put him out of her mind until Friday!

Friday. Pippi had never looked forward to a dinner engagement with such foreboding. Her stomach felt tied in knots as she tore lettuce for the tossed green salad she planned to bring.

She glanced nervously at the pan of dark spicy old-fashioned gingerbread cooling on the counter. Maybe it was a mistake to bring both a salad and a dessert. What was Mary going to think about a woman who turned up at Jeremy's place alone, loaded down with food just to "help out?"

"I know what *I'd* think," she said aloud to the salad bowl. "I'd think that woman had a crush on Jeremy the size of Texas, and not enough pride or sense to hide it!" The mortifying part was that she'd be at least half right.

But it was too late to worry about that now. Jeremy was so nervous and keyed-up over this dinner that he'd probably go quietly berserk if she showed up with only a salad and no dessert. After all their consultations over the phone about the menu, the wine, and even how he should set the table, Pippi couldn't let him down like that.

When the salad was ready except for the dressing, she put it into the refrigerator and whisked off her apron. Time for one last critical inspection in the mirror before she left.

She looked a little pale, even wearing extra makeup. But her trim navy dress slacks and delicate, filigree-patterned cotton sweater were thoroughly appropriate for the occasion. No one could accuse her of dressing to compete for male attention. Yet she hoped she looked good enough so that no one would *dare* feel sorry for her.

"And I'd better not catch you feeling sorry for yourself!" she warned her reflection. "The whole idea is to take your nasty medicine tonight, so that tomorrow you'll wake up cured."

She tossed her coppery red curls defiantly as she met the sad, skeptical look in her own blue eyes. "That's right—*cured!*" she insisted belligerently.

Still the eyes were full of disbelief, and she grimaced ruefully. "Well, convalescing, anyway," she compromised.

"What do you mean, you've had a few cancellations?" The salad bowl almost slid off the pan of gingerbread and onto the floor as Pippi came to an abrupt halt in Jeremy's immaculate, airy, white-tiled kitchen. The room was bathed in sunset glow from the overhead skylight, which no doubt explained the pink tinge on Jeremy's cheeks.

"Larry and Brenda Sommers decided to stay home with the baby, who just came down with strep throat. Bob Patterson missed a connecting flight and won't be home until midnight, so his wife isn't coming either. And Jan and Peter both have the flu. That leaves just you and me and Mary."

"How cozy," Pippi murmured in a strangled voice. This couldn't be happening. It was like something out of a surrealistic horror movie. A very low-budget surrealistic horror movie.

Jeremy looked flustered, and no wonder. His carefully planned dinner party had been reduced to a shambles. But his evening could still be saved, Pippi decided.

"I'll leave these here and go on home," she announced, setting the food on the counter. "That way, you and Mary can have a nice, romantic dinner for two."

"No, Pip—stay!"

"But it'll be so awkward . . ." The thought of spending the evening alone with Jeremy and Mary made her shudder. If that was the cure, she preferred the disease. "No, I can't stay."

She was heading for the door when two things happened at once. A kettle boiled over on the stove and the phone rang.

"Will you get that?" Jeremy asked distractedly as he rushed to move the pan and turn down the burner.

Pippi picked up the phone and, before she could speak, a woman's voice said urgently, "Jeremy, this is Mary."

"I'm afraid Jeremy's busy in the kitchen right this minute," Pippi hastily informed the caller, feeling an unpleasant tightness in her throat. So this was Mary. This human, audible voice. Soft and musical, but undeniably real.

"Who is it?" Jeremy asked, having solved the minor crisis on the stovetop.

"Mary." Pippi handed him the receiver and turned to beat a hasty retreat. But Jeremy caught her arm in a deceptively mild grip and held her there.

"Hello, Mary," he said in that subtly alluring

voice he'd first practiced on Pippi only the week before. "Running late?"

Mary's reply seemed to take quite a while, and Pippi squirmed, trying to free her arm so she could leave the room.

"Of course I understand," Jeremy said at last in a strained voice. "We can have dinner another time. Don't worry about it—it's no trouble. Have a nice weekend. 'Bye."

His body was stiff with tension as he hung up. Pippi could feel it running through the strong fingers laced around her arm.

"It seems Mary has an unexpected visitor from out of town this weekend. An old friend from college," he explained tersely.

"Male or female?" Pippi asked as indignation began to boil inside her at such cavalier treatment of Jeremy. Indignation, and a guilty sense of relief that she didn't have to face Mary tonight after all.

"I didn't ask."

"It makes me so mad! After you worked so hard on this damn dinner, which was all my idea in the first place! Jeremy, I'm sorry." She laid her hand on his shoulder in a gesture of comfort and remorse.

The contact of her palm against his tense, steely flesh instantly drew her again into the dizzying vortex of her own unconfessed desires. The swiftness and strength of the sweet sensations ripping through her body took her breath away.

But Jeremy sensed none of this. He just patted her hand and said, "Don't blame yourself, Pip. Nobody could have predicted that all my invited guests would stay away in droves." He laughed. "My cooking must be worse than I thought!"

She cautiously withdrew her hand and stepped

back. "There's nothing wrong with your cooking," she insisted.

"It's good to hear you say that, since I'm counting on you to stay and help devour all this food I've got ready!"

She hesitated. Of course Char would have told her to get the hell out of there. The last thing she needed was to spend more time alone with Jeremy. But she couldn't abandon him in the midst of his disappointment, or in the midst of nine servings of boneless chicken breast, for that matter.

"I'll stay," she said.

"Wonderful." There was a look in his eyes as if he really meant it, and Pippi felt a warm glow inside. Even if she couldn't have his love, she had his deep and abiding friendship. It wasn't enough, but it was better than nothing.

The food was delicious. "It's a good thing those party poopers all stayed home so we could have second helpings of everything!" Jeremy joked as he spooned another dollop of freshly whipped cream onto his square of gingerbread.

Pippi laughed. There was so much happiness in being with Jeremy, sharing good food and talk and wine and laughter. Tomorrow was soon enough to worry about falling out of love with him. For now she wanted to savor their closeness. Never mind whether it was the wise thing to do. It was what she wanted. Period.

"Shall we see if it's warm enough to sit out on the deck?" he suggested.

"Good idea." They carried their coffee cups and dessert plates out the sliding glass doors onto the broad redwood deck that ran the entire length of the house.

It was a balmy spring night. The air was full of

the scent of blossoms and newly mown grass. A warm breeze rustled in the birches along the shore of the small lake behind the house.

"It's beautiful," Pippi said, sinking onto a padded lounge chair and leaning back to gaze up at the stars.

"Yes," Jeremy said in a soft, husky voice. He turned away quickly, as if overcome with sudden emotion.

Pippi sat very still, imagining the regret he must be feeling because Mary wasn't with him. It was a night made for lovers. And he was stuck with just a friend. She sighed.

"I'll turn up the music," he said, stepping back inside.

Pippi closed her eyes as the moody, suggestive rhythm of a jazz piano swirled about her. Her senses were drowning in the poignant beauty of the night. But it was a cruel beauty, because it made her ache for something, someone, she couldn't have.

She didn't hear Jeremy come back outside. The first she knew of his return was when the warmth of his hip and thigh pressed against her leg as he sat down beside her on the lounge chair.

Her pulse skyrocketed. Her breath was trapped in her throat. Her whole body was suddenly tingling with electricity. He took her hand and threaded his fingers through hers.

"I need your advice again, Pip." His voice was troubled. "I don't know where to go from here."

She took a deep breath and drew her hand out of his. Once again she'd let her imagination take off into the stratosphere, and once again she'd been brought down to earth with a painful thud.

"You mean . . . with Mary?" she managed to ask,

her voice shaking just a little. What a moronic question! Of course he meant with Mary.

"I'm not sure the plan is working," he said. "Sometimes I think it must be working, it has to be, I can almost see it in her eyes! But then, other times, I'm sure it's *not*. How can I know, dammit?"

Pippi was silent. She didn't want to be discouraging, but it seemed obvious to her that "the plan" was a failure. Mary's behavior tonight made that clear. Any woman who would back out of a dinner with Jeremy at the last minute just because a friend happened to be in town was not on the brink of falling in love with him.

"Listen, Pip," he said urgently. "Don't you think it's time I came right out and told her how I feel?"

"No!" Her answer was instinctive, but she didn't stop to think whether it was based on the facts of the case or just on her own wishes.

"Then what should I do? You've counseled me to be subtle, but subtlety doesn't seem to be getting the job done."

"True." She folded her arms across her chest and tried to think, which was damnably hard to do with Jeremy so temptingly close in the velvet darkness. She didn't like where her thoughts were taking her either. She didn't like it at all.

"It's time to make your move," she said at last, trying not to sound as unhappy about it as she felt.

"My move?"

"Yes. A direct attempt at seduction. You've laid the foundation. Now build on it."

"Seduction? But isn't that what I've been trying all along? All those little tricks you taught me, that we practiced together?"

Her throaty laugh felt like sandpaper along the length of her vocal cords. "That was only the beginning, Jeremy! You started off by tempting and tantalizing her with *possibilities*. Now you've got to show her you want those possibilities to become reality."

"You mean . . ."

Couldn't he figure out what she was trying to say without making her spell it out for him? The darkness hid the single teardrop that trickled down her cheek, but it couldn't hide the husky tremor in her voice. "Seduce her for real this time," she said.

Stunned silence. It was impossible to guess what Jeremy was thinking, though he was so near she could hear the sudden acceleration of his quiet breathing.

"There's just one problem, Pip."

"Mmm?" she murmured, afraid he'd hear the tears in her voice if she spoke.

He cleared his throat. "I've never—um—*seduced* anyone before."

"*What?*" She gasped incredulously. "Jeremy Holt! If you expect me to believe you're a thirty-two-year-old vir—"

"Hardly," he broke in, laughing. "All I'm saying is that I've never seduced anyone."

"Oh, sure. You're so irresistible that all you have to do is whistle and women come running. Why waste your time seducing them?"

"I didn't mean it like that!" he exclaimed in exasperation. "Listen. Ever since I outgrew the teenage phase of making out in the backseat of my car—and I would *not* dignify what went on there with so flattering a label as 'seduction'—my relationships with women have been based on *mutual* feelings."

"But, Jeremy—"

"Let me finish. If a relationship is developing and deepening naturally, there's no need to seduce anyone. There just comes a point when two caring, intelligent people both know that sexual intimacy is the next step." A note of uncertainty entered his voice. "Of course, sometimes there are complications. . . ."

"Ah-ha! And your complication is that Mary seems to be a little slow in getting the message! Don't you see, that's where seduction comes in handy? To speed things up."

After a slight pause Jeremy spoke, sounding very thoughtful indeed. "You're saying, then, that I could bring about that moment of mutual understanding a lot quicker if I used physical persuasion?"

"Precisely." Pippi felt a momentary triumph at having made her point, but then realization struck. What was she *doing*, encouraging him like this? She didn't want him to convince Mary that sexual intimacy was *their* next step.

"On the other hand," she added hastily, "sometimes a relationship is all wrong from the start, and there's never going to be mutual anything. In that case, the one holding back is showing good judgment and you'll just make an awful mess if you start pushing."

"A sobering thought." He sighed. "But it's a risk I'll have to take, because you're right. It's time for me to make my move."

Damn! "Are you sure?" she asked desperately. Her and her big mouth! She had only herself to blame.

"Oh, yes. I'm very sure. How can this relationship be anything but right? We were meant for each other." The deep-timbred certainty in his voice reverberated through her. His face, veiled by the night, was only inches from her own.

"But maybe if you wait just a little longer . . ."

"No. No more waiting. I want to make love to the woman I love! I want to hold her naked in my arms and taste her sweet fire." His voice was hoarse with emotion. "And I'll go mad if it doesn't happen soon."

The intimacy of his words sent a dagger of pain through Pippi. She spoke with brisk, embarrassed awkwardness. "Well, then. Your mind's made up."

"Definitely." The single, fervent word hung in the air like a dark, velvety moth on the wing.

"So that's that."

"Not quite." Some new quality in his voice sent a quiver up her spine. She noticed a perceptible tensing of his thigh muscles where his leg pressed against her own.

"What do you mean?"

"I need your help, Pip. As I said, I've never seduced anyone before. I could use a few pointers."

"But . . . that's ridiculous!"

"Pip! I never thought *you* would make fun of my ignorance and inexperience," he said in a hurt voice that couldn't possibly be sincere. Or could it? In the darkness she wasn't able to tell for sure.

"Of course I'm not making fun of you!" she snapped. "But not for one second do I believe that you're ignorant enough to need any advice from me on how to seduce a woman into your bed!" Her voice choked a little as she blurted out the honest truth. "Just follow your instincts and you'll do fine."

She had to get out of there. She swung both legs over the side of the lounge chair and tried to scramble to her feet. She couldn't budge though, because Jeremy's hands were suddenly circling her narrow waist.

His laced fingers seared her like flame through her delicate sweater. "Wait," he said in a feather-soft voice that set all her senses stirring. "Tell me more. I should follow my instincts . . . how?"

Pippi couldn't have answered him just then if her life depended on it. It took all her self-control to hide what was happening inside her in response to his touch.

"Did you mean like this?" he asked, abruptly pulling her against him and enveloping her mouth with his in a rough, thorough, feverish kiss.

"No!" She turned her head away frantically, but not before the hard, exciting pressure of his mouth had launched a dozen skyrockets deep within her.

"That's the wrong approach, huh? Too crude, you think?" he asked anxiously.

"Mmm," she agreed in a dazed murmur. "Much too crude."

"Then how about this?" One hand cupped the nape of her neck and his fingers entwined in her soft, luxuriant curls. With his other hand he slowly traced the satiny skin of her brow and temple.

She tried to shake her head, but the light, sensuous touch of his fingertips mesmerized her. And then his thumb descended to brush the crest of her cheekbone, and he discovered the moist traces of her earlier tears.

"Pip?" His voice was troubled.

"It's this darn hay fever!" she exclaimed with desperate resourcefulness. "Something in the air tonight is making my eyes water and . . . *ah-ah-choo!*" The faked sneeze added a very convincing touch to the lie, she thought. "Hadn't we better go inside?"

"We will in just a minute." He bent his head and softly kissed the wetness from her cheeks. His lips drifted down to the curve of her mouth, where he placed the merest whisper of a honeyed kiss. And then, a heartbeat later, another. And another.

His tongue slipped silkenly between her lips at

the exact moment his hand stroked down her neck and kept on going.

"No!" The protest she should have uttered much sooner was wrenched from her lips as she felt his palm graze the fullness of her breast. "This is all wrong!"

Jeremy drew back, breathing hard. "*Damn.* Here I thought I was finally getting the hang of it, and now you tell me I'm *still* going at it wrong!"

Pippi was speechless. Did he honestly think she was trying to offer him advice on his technique?

"Please tell me what to do!" he pleaded. "But for heaven's sake, don't tell me to follow my instincts! That's what I've just been doing, and obviously it's not working."

She knew there wasn't a damn thing wrong with his instincts, but he sure had a warped sense of what was acceptable behavior between friends. How dare he use her as a guinea pig like this? And why was she letting him get away with it?

"You might try *talking* to her first instead of attacking her like a swarm of hungry locusts," she said a bit curtly. "And stop prac—"

"Talk to her?" he interrupted. "Seductively, you mean?" Without waiting for an answer he began to experiment. "You are so beautiful tonight," he whispered.

"Give me a break. It's so dark out here you can't even *see* me!" Pippi pointed out.

"But your image is branded on my senses by an eternal flame. And tonight the magic of your nearness makes that image glow so brightly, it dazzles me."

"Are you making this up off the top of your head?" she asked, awestruck.

"I'm not making anything up." His hands slipped beneath the hem of her sweater and clasped the taut, bare flesh of her lower rib cage. He eased her backward until she was reclining against the lounge chair.

"But . . ."

"Your eyes are full of starlight," he murmured. His dark silhouette hovered over her, only inches away, and his deep, vibrant voice wove a potent spell of enchantment. "Your hair smells like lilacs."

Now was definitely the time to make another smart, cynical remark, but Pippi couldn't think of a thing to say.

"I always dreamed how your skin would feel against my cheek," he breathed. "Soft and silky as rose petals." His face lowered to hers and his hard, clean-shaven jaw reverently brushed her cheek. "And it does. It *does.*"

His lips tasted the creamy curve of her neck, then dropped down to string a necklace of jewel-like, precious kisses along the skin above the scalloped edge of her sweater.

Pippi could not restrain a murmured sigh of pleasure as wave upon wave of warm desire coursed through her body. Instantly, Jeremy's mouth fitted over hers, drinking in the small earthy sound of her delight.

His hands moved higher underneath her sweater until his thumbs stroked the underside of her breasts. Deep within her mouth his tongue probed her sweetness with a rhythm that matched the exploratory caress of his hands.

Her hips arched upward against him, and she felt how the hard thrust of his arousal tautened the fabric of his trousers. Despite the layers of their clothing, their bodies made intimate contact as his hardness pressed into her soft hollows.

He pushed her sweater up over her breasts, folding it back from her naked skin as if he were peeling a ripe, tempting piece of fruit. Then he undid the clasp of her bra.

"I've been hungry for this for so long," he said, then licked the hard, delicate buds of her nipples. Pippi whimpered with ecstasy and gripped his shoulders as the warm, liquid pressure of his mouth closed fiercely over first one bare breast, then the other.

When he lifted his head, the night air felt suddenly cool against her dampened, sensitized flesh.

"Let's go inside and turn on the lights," he said huskily. "Now that I finally have you in my arms, I want to see your beautiful body the first time we make love together."

His words snapped her out of the warm haze of never-never land into the pain and ugliness of reality. She sat up, not saying a word as her trembling fingers refastened her bra and tugged down her sweater.

"Pip . . ."

"Whose body do you expect to see once the lights go on?" she asked bitterly. "Mine . . . or Mary's?"

"What the hell is that supposed to mean?"

"Isn't it obvious? You were pretending I was Mary just now. Everything you said and did was meant for her."

He didn't bother to deny her accusation, but the air rattled out of his lungs in one incredulous gust. "Oh, hell. I don't believe this!" He jumped to his feet and began pacing restlessly back and forth until his footsteps halted in mid-stride. "There's only one way to clear up this little misunderstanding," he said. "Pip, I—"

She gasped. "*Little misunderstanding?* You bastard! You know perfectly well you're in love with Mary, yet you tried to seduce me! I don't call that a little misunderstanding, Jeremy. I call it a betrayal."

Leaving him standing there speechless, she fled into the house, scooped up her purse, and slammed the front door behind her as she raced for her car.

"Pip, *wait!*" Jeremy shouted after her as she started the engine. But there was no way she could bear to face him again tonight, not with tears of shame and anger and heartbreak pouring down her cheeks.

She pulled away so fast, the tires squealed.

Eight

Pippi had to stop on the side of the road more than once to wipe away tears that made it hazardous to drive.

"I never needed windshield wipers on my *eyes* before!" she muttered, and glanced at her watch. It felt like the middle of the night, but it wasn't even eleven yet. In fact, it was still early enough to—

"No," she said emphatically. "You are a mature, independent, capable adult. You can handle this without calling your mother!" Besides, Mom was so unpredictable. You never knew how she might react to things.

But the minute Pippi walked into her apartment she headed straight for the phone. "Hi, Dad. Is Mom still up?" she asked in a quavery voice when her stepfather answered.

"She's in the shower. Pippi, are you all right? You sound a bit . . ."

Pippi tried to say she was fine, but it came out as a muffled sob.

"Hold on, honey. I'll get your mother."

Seconds later her mother's worried voice said, "Pippi? What's happened?"

"Oh, *Mom*!" Pippi choked out. "It's so good to hear your voice."

"There, there, honey. Tell me what's wrong. Is it Jeremy?"

Pippi started to cry again at the mention of his name. "Yes." She sniffled. "Did Char tell you . . ." Her voice was wavering so much she couldn't continue.

"Char told me all about Jeremy. But what's he done now to get you so upset? Did he get engaged to that other girl?"

"N-no." Pippi took several deep, shaky breaths, trying to prepare herself to deliver the shocking truth. "He tried to make love to me."

The silence at the other end of the line went on so long, Pippi began to fear her mother had fainted dead away. When the older woman spoke at last, she sounded very confused.

"But . . . isn't that a good sign? After all, he can't be too serious about this other girl if he's making a pass at *you*, now, can he?"

"Oh, Mom. You don't understand."

"That's for sure. There must be a few things you're not telling me."

So Pippi tried to explain. How she'd offered to help Jeremy court the woman he loved. How she'd taught him to dance, and how he'd taken her out for a "dress rehearsal." How she'd gone up in a glider with him and come down realizing she was in love with him. How she'd tried to cure herself by instigating tonight's dinner party, an effort that failed when all the guests, including Mary, canceled at the last minute.

The next part was the hardest to explain to her

mother. How Jeremy had asked her to give him a few pointers on seduction. "Of course I told him no," Pippi said. "But he kept misunderstanding me. And before I knew it, he was doing an experimental seduction on me, like I was a laboratory rat or something!"

"That should be 'as if I *were* a laboratory rat,' dear," her mother informed her placidly.

"Mom!" Pippi wailed. "I was hoping for a little sympathy from you, not a grammar lesson! Don't you understand? I was darn near seduced tonight by a man who was pretending I was somebody else! He was making love to the image of another woman, not to me." The tears began falling again.

Her mother's reply was prompt and succinct. "Poppycock."

"I beg your pardon?"

"You heard me, dear. Poppycock. Men don't make love to images! They make love to flesh-and-blood women. And bodies don't pretend, even if people do. If Jeremy was making love to you, it means his body wants yours, and no pretense about it!"

"What good is that when he's in love with another woman?" Pippi sobbed. "I can't believe my own mother—"

"And *I* can't believe my own daughter has saw-dust in her head instead of brains! What makes you so sure Jeremy is in love with this Mary person?"

"B-because he told me so."

"You're very trusting." It was obviously not meant as a compliment. "I, on the other hand, have all kinds of suspicions about what is really going on here. But never mind that now. Just look at it this way. What if Jeremy is mistaken about his feelings? What if he only *thinks* he's in love with her?"

It was a mind-boggling thought. And much too good to be true. "That's im—"

"But how well does he really know this girl?" her mother jumped in like a prosecuting attorney cross-examining a hostile witness. "Does he share with her the kind of close, supportive friendship he has with you? Do they laugh at the same jokes? Does—"

"But that's the whole problem, Mom!" Pippi interrupted impatiently. "He thinks of me as just a friend. Not someone to fall in love with."

"Was he thinking of you as just a friend tonight?" her mother countered ruthlessly.

Pippi gulped. "I guess not. But—"

"Well, then! You've got everything going for you. He likes you and he wants you. Jeremy's not stupid—it won't take him long to figure out it's only logical to *love* you too. Especially if you give him a little encouragement."

"Mom!" Pippi exclaimed, hardly able to believe her ears. Was this really her mother talking? "The man happens to be in love with someone else!"

"So you keep telling me, dear." Inexplicably, her mother laughed, a tinkling, silvery sound. "But even if he does have a superficial infatuation for another girl, that's no reason to give up. He'll come to his senses sooner or later. Just make him forget her."

"Easy for you to say."

"Easy for you to *do* if she keeps giving him the cold shoulder the way she's been doing. From the sound of it, he's barely gotten to first base with her."

Pippi, who'd been perched on the arm of her living room sofa, toppled backward into its cushioned depths, bringing the phone clanging down onto the floor beside her. "Mom! I've never heard you talk like this!"

"There's nothing wrong with using a pithy, well-chosen slang expression to emphasize a point. As long as it's done in good taste."

"I'll bear that in mind."

"Good. And here's something else to bear in mind—if you don't quit playing cupid for Jeremy and that rival of yours, you're either a scoundrel or a fool!"

"Huh?"

"You're a scoundrel if you sabotage his courtship by giving bad advice, but you're a total fool if you work against yourself by giving good advice. So tell him you're off the case."

"I was planning to. *If* I ever speak to him again, that is."

"Of course you'll speak to him. How can he tell you he loves you if you're not even on speaking terms?"

"Oh, Mom." Pippi laughed. "You're such an optimist."

"I just want you to be happy," her mother said gruffly. "I've been worried about you. All those selfish young men you kept insisting you were in love with. The truth is, dear, they reminded me of your father. And I hated to see you make the same mistakes I did back when I was too young and naive to know better."

"Omigosh," Pippi whispered. "Freud would have a field day with this one."

"Leave *him* out of this, for heaven's sake! You've got enough to worry about with making sure Jeremy tries to make love to you again. Only this time don't run off in a huff right when it starts to get interesting."

"Mom!"

"Good night, dear. Call again if you need more advice." And she hung up.

Good old Mom. Calling her with a problem was like jumping into a rushing stream of ice-cold mountain spring water. It left you slightly dazed and gasping for breath, but it sure was invigorating. No doubt about that.

Their conversation had given Pippi a lot to think about, so she stayed awake, thinking, until well after midnight. But not once did she feel like crying. She was too busy making plans.

But someone else was making plans as well.

Pippi had just finished dressing for racquetball the next morning—after all, it *was* Saturday—when the downstairs buzzer rang. It was Jeremy.

Waiting for him to climb the stairs to her apartment, Pippi felt as if all her pulse points must be visibly throbbing with suspense. And the sight of his tall, lean figure caused her to practically melt against the doorjamb. How had she ever been content with mere friendship from this man?

His face looked pale and stern and determined. But his eyes were troubled and vulnerable beneath their silky lashes.

"We need to talk," he said.

"I agree. Come on in." Her knees were trembling as she led the way into the apartment.

The first thing Jeremy saw was Pippi's canvas tote bag of racquetball gear packed and ready by the door.

"I completely forgot!" he said, turning to her with a look of puzzled surprise on his face. "Were you actually planning to show up for our match this morning . . . just as if nothing had happened?"

"Why not?" she answered with smiling nonchalance and a racing pulse. "What exactly *did* happen, in your opinion?"

"You know damn well what happened." His jaw jutted out at a hard angle, and his arm and shoulder muscles were corded with tension under his pale blue knit shirt. "What *almost* happened," he amended. "We almost became lovers. But you accused me of pretending you were Mary. And then you ran off—"

"In a huff," Pippi interjected helpfully, quoting her mother.

"—before I could tell you . . ."

"Tell me what?" Pippi prompted him as his sentence trailed off into an uncertain silence and his ears turned bright red.

"That I wasn't pretending."

Pippi's mouth fell open with shock. Was he saying what she hoped he was saying? Could Mom have been right after all? "Omigosh, I think I'd better sit down!" She staggered over to the sofa and collapsed into a sitting position. "Now. Say that again?"

"I wasn't pretending, Pip. I knew all along it was you I was touching, you I was kissing, and you I wanted to make love to. And I'm afraid I loved every minute of it!" he finished defiantly.

"You did?" Pippi breathed, trying to keep her reckless hopes from running away with her. "But . . . what about Mary?"

He sighed, and his gaze shifted uneasily away from her as he replied. "I've been awake all night asking myself that very question, Pip. And a hundred other questions besides. But I honestly don't know the answers. I think you and I both need some time to adjust to this."

"I see." She tried to keep the disappointment out

of her voice. Had she actually hoped to hear him say he'd fallen out of love, all in one night, with the woman he'd adored so faithfully for months? And would she still want him if he were that fickle? She took a sidelong glance at the taut, uneasy stance of his proud, strong body. Whom did she think she was kidding? Of course she would still want him.

"What about you and Marc?" Jeremy asked gruffly. "Are you still sure about your feelings for him after the way you responded to me last night?"

Silence seemed the safest answer, but her flushed cheeks and downcast eyes spoke for her.

Jeremy smiled a wry, gentle smile. "So, it seems last night turned things upside down for both of us. Now all we have to do is figure out what it all means. Luckily, I have a plan."

"A plan?" Her voice faltered. Oh, dear, not another *plan*.

"My family owns an old log cabin on the Mississippi River northeast of Brainerd. It's primitive, but peaceful. Will you drive up there with me today so we can spend the weekend sorting out our feelings?"

Pippi stared at him. He was handing it to her on a silver platter. The chance of a lifetime. The chance to make him forget Mary and fall in love with her, Pippi Smith.

But, like every chance, this one carried the risk of failure. There was no guarantee that when Jeremy's feelings were all neatly sorted out he'd find himself in love with Pippi. But she would do her damndest to make sure he was!

She was so caught up in her thoughts that she forgot to say yes. Jeremy's expression grew more and more anxious with every passing second.

"Why is it such a tough decision, Pip? I'm not asking you to go to bed with me, just to—"

"You're *not*?" she broke in, startled. When he'd invited her to go away with him for the weekend, naturally she'd just assumed . . .

"Of course not. Haven't I just been saying we need time to discover how we really feel about each other? The last thing I'd want to do is pressure you into something you're not ready for."

"Oh." Why did he have to be so damn noble? Nothing was going to stop *her* from trying to pressure him into loving her, whether he was ready for it or not!

"So you'll come to the cabin?" he continued. "I promise you won't have to fear a repeat of last night. That only happened because I got caught off guard by my own response." He gave an apologetic chuckle. "It seems my hormones are a bit over-active after all these months of carrying the torch for a woman who thought of me as just a friend."

Pippi bit her lip at the reminder of his strong attachment to Mary. Could she really hope to take Mary's place as the "one woman" in the heart of this "one-woman man"? Yes, she could. Because Mary hadn't had the brains to love him back! And Pippi had so much love to give him that he couldn't possibly stay immune.

"Yes, I'll go to the cabin with you," she said. But she added a silent promise of her own. No matter what Jeremy intended, last night was *definitely* going to be repeated. Only this time, taking Mom's advice, she wouldn't run off in a huff just when things got interesting!

It took Pippi longer to pack for the weekend with Jeremy than it had taken her to pack for her six-week vacation in Europe.

She agonized over which of three nightgowns was the most alluring and provocative, and ended up packing all three. She debated over what shade of lipstick to wear, whether her perfume for the occasion should be sultry and exotic or delicate and floral, and whether she should drop everything and paint her toenails a bright, passionate red.

In the end, her makeup case weighed a ton and contained enough cosmetics to embellish all the contestants in a national beauty contest. She threw in bottles and tubes she hadn't opened for years. She even packed an eyelash curler, a gadget she hadn't used since the days when she was first dating her ex-husband, Stephen.

Her suitcase was crammed with outfits she was bringing "just in case." Just in case she finally made up her mind and decided which one to wear!

She sank down onto her bed amid the wild disarray of her packing and felt like bursting into tears. This was ridiculous! Why couldn't she decide on such a simple thing as what color sweater to wear?

"Because I'm scared to death at the thought of being 'on trial' the whole darn weekend!" she muttered. She wanted so desperately to make a good impression. One that would convince Jeremy to fall in love with her. But what if she slipped up on some tiny detail that could have made all the difference? What if she blew her chances by wearing lemon yellow just when she could have won Jeremy's heart forever if only she'd worn midnight blue?

"Augh! That's the stupidest thing I ever heard!" she informed herself crossly. "If Jeremy discovers he loves me, it'll be because I'm *me*, not because I'm wearing a blue sweater!"

So she decided to flip a coin and pack just the bare minimum. But at that very minute her doorbell rang. Of course it was Jeremy, back already with his car carefully loaded with groceries and supplies, ready to go. So of course Pippi said she was ready too.

He blinked at the sight of her large, bulging suitcase and matching makeup case. "Looks like you're ready for anything!" he teased.

Pippi wanted to sink through the floor. What had she been thinking of? Nobody but a real space case would pack this much for a two-day trip to a cabin in the woods. Jeremy was never going to fall in love with her if she kept acting like an idiot.

But he didn't utter a word of complaint or criticism. After he had painstakingly rearranged the contents of his car to accommodate all her luggage, they set off. Pippi clenched her hands in her lap and tried to think of something—anything!—to say to break the awkward silence.

It was hard for her to remember they had once been friends who shared a comfortable, confiding, joking relationship. Now they were like two nervous strangers. Jeremy seemed even more ill-at-ease than on that fateful day when he had first told her about Mary. Maybe, Pippi thought, he was already regretting this trip to the cabin with her. Maybe he'd already decided that last night was a total mistake but he was too embarrassed tell her. Maybe . . .

But things went from bad to worse. It was after they'd already been driving for twenty minutes that Pippi remembered what she'd forgotten to pack. She had brought enough extra clothes to last a week, enough cosmetics to last a year, and enough luggage to tour the world, but still she'd left something behind. Something important. Something no woman planning a seduction should be without. Her birth control pills.

She groaned and covered her face with her hands.

"Jeremy, we have to turn around," she said in a small, miserable voice.

He screeched to a stop at the side of the road and turned to face her. His expression was so grim, she shrank back in fright. "Why?" he demanded harshly.

"B-because I forgot . . . something." She blushed guiltily at the thought of just what she'd forgotten and why she hoped she would need them.

"What?"

"S-something I'll need this weekend."

"Oh. Can't we buy a replacement at one of the stores on the way?" He watched her anxiously, almost suspiciously.

She went redder still. "N-no. We have to go back." She stared down at her lap, wishing she could give him an explanation, but not willing to risk telling him the truth.

"Then we'll go back." With a vicious wrench of the steering wheel he spun the car into a U-turn that sent them roaring back over the miles they'd just covered. His face was white with anger, and Pippi's heart sank.

When they pulled up in front of her house, Jeremy didn't say a word. "I'll be right back," she promised nervously.

"Will you?" The hard, cynical inflection of his voice made it sound as if he didn't care if she never came back at all.

She was practically crying as she raced up the stairs to her apartment. This was awful. Jeremy was furious with her, and no wonder. Why had she picked today to fall apart? Where was the well-organized, competent, efficient person she used to be?

It took only seconds to find the pills and tuck them into her purse. But it took considerably longer to find something that would serve as her excuse for making Jeremy turn around and drive all the way back. The answer, when it occurred to her at last, was so obvious, she felt like a moron for not thinking of it sooner. Her camera. She'd forgotten to take her camera.

With the carrying case slung over her shoulder, she hurried downstairs and back out to the car. She bit her lip at what she saw there. Jeremy's head was bent over the wheel as if he were in the last throes of wrathful impatience.

"I forgot my camera," she announced breathlessly as she slipped into her seat.

His head came up with a jerk. One instant his eyes were bleak and empty, and then they were full of astonishment. "You're back!" He sounded relieved. "And you really did forget something." He started to laugh.

"Of course I'm back. And of course I really forgot something! You don't think I'd make you turn around for *nothing*, do you?"

"Oh, Pip. Do you realize I've been sitting out here wondering how you intended to break it to me that you weren't coming to the cabin after all? The minute you asked me to turn around, I was sure you'd changed your mind about the whole weekend."

She stared at him with her mouth open. "But why would you think that? Of course I want to come! You're the one who's been acting like you're sorry you even suggested the idea!"

He gave her a big, tight-lipped, embarrassed grin. "Hell, no!" he muttered. "I've just been acting scared. I want this weekend with you more than anything."

"Oh. Well, then." She felt the hard coil of tension inside her unwind by several notches. Her lips curved in a smile. "What are we waiting for?"

She heard his breath catch. His brown eyes were murky and bemused with emotion as he lifted his hand to her face. The tip of his finger brushed lightly along the smiling fullness of her mouth.

"I love your smile," he whispered huskily, and Pippi wanted him to put his arms around her and kiss her senseless. She thought for an instant that he might.

But then he blushed and drew his hand away. He concentrated intently on turning the key in the ignition. "Sorry about that," he muttered.

"Don't be." But she whispered it so bashfully that he must not have heard. They drove north in silence, each intensely aware of the other, each filled with hopes and fears for what might happen in the hours ahead.

Nine

The trouble started when they turned off the highway onto the narrow, muddy track to the cabin.

Springtime was not as advanced this far north as it was in the Twin Cities. Through the trunks of the tall dark pines growing along the road Pippi glimpsed patches of snow, still unmelted, lurking in the perpetual shade beneath the trees.

The ground was saturated with water from the recent spring thaw. At first the track was merely difficult to drive on. Soon it became impossible. Rather than venture through the next series of treacherously deep ruts filled with water, Jeremy stopped the car.

"I don't want to risk getting us stuck back here," he said. "Damn! I'd forgotten the road was this bad."

"What are we going to do?"

"We'll have to walk the rest of the way. Luckily it's less than a mile to the cabin from here."

Less than a mile? Pippi glanced down at her fashionable high-heeled suede boots and cringed.

Those boots were meant for dry city pavements, not muddy roads. And what about all her luggage?

"Looks like we'll be making a couple of trips," Jeremy said, casting a dubious eye over the car's contents. "I'd better sort out what's absolutely essential, like drinking water, sleeping bags, flashlights, food, and insect repellent."

Pippi gulped. When Jeremy said this place was primitive, he obviously hadn't been kidding. "I'll sort through my stuff and see what I can do without," she volunteered in a small voice.

"Thanks, Pip. I knew I could count on you." His smile of approval helped her face the sad task of rummaging through all the impractical finery she had packed and selecting just one change of clothes for the next morning.

After adding a few basic toiletries from her makeup case, she still had some space left in the brown paper sack that now served as her "luggage." She shot a glance at Jeremy to make sure he wasn't watching, then sneaked a slinky little nightshirt of pure white silk into the bag.

"I've whittled it down to the bare essentials," she proudly informed Jeremy.

"Great, Pip. Do you have any room in that sack for the can opener and the matches and a roll of toilet paper?" She nodded. "How about a pound of raw steak?"

"No!"

"How about a couple of onions?"

"Oh, all right." And if her sexy nightgown ended up smelling like onions, well, that was just the price she would have to pay for trying to seduce somebody in the wilderness.

Jeremy was worried.

He couldn't help but fear that bringing Pippi to

the cabin would turn out to be the biggest mistake of his life. The hike in from the car was a disaster. After gallantly leaving behind most of her luggage, Pippi had insisted on shouldering a load that was far too heavy for her. And she'd airily dismissed all his protests, claiming she wanted to get this over with in one trip, not two.

The mud was almost up to her knees. Jeremy winced, watching her struggle through it. He knew her feet must be killing her in those ridiculous high-heeled boots, and her slender shoulders were probably aching. But she held her curly red head defiantly erect, and never once did her plucky, cheerful grin seem to falter.

Belatedly, he tried to prepare her for the Spartan condition of the cabin. No running water, no electricity, an ancient wood-burning stove. And no doubt the place would be musty and damp after being closed up all winter.

She just laughed her low, musical, husky laugh. "Does the outhouse have a genuine half moon over the door?" she asked.

He had to confess that it did not.

"Darn. I've always wanted to try one of those. What's the half moon for anyway?"

"I'm afraid I don't know." He felt an absurd regret that he had neither a half moon nor an answer for her. Under her brave, determined front, he could see she was tense and exhausted. Damn this wet, muddy road! And damn him for forgetting what it could be like this time of year.

He breathed a sigh of relief when they finally waded out of the low, marshy area and saw the cabin basking serenely in the late afternoon sunshine. It was as beautiful as he remembered it. The dark brown, tree-fringed river flowed just a stone's throw away from the cabin door, curving in a loop that encircled and protected these few acres so that they were almost like an island set apart from the world.

Jeremy's great-uncle Matthew had built the cabin in the early days of the twentieth century. Its logs and stones had weathered nearly eight decades of fierce northern winters. Jeremy loved the place.

Still, he'd been a fool to bring Pippi here. How could this weekend bring them closer together if they had to wage a constant struggle against physical hardship and discomfort? He should have picked a place with paved roads and indoor plumbing!

And no wood ticks.

"Jeremy, what are these awful creepy-crawly things that keep dropping out of the trees on me?" Pippi asked in a tremulous voice.

"Oh, damn." Disaster! His brains must have been out to lunch when he planned this trip! How could he have forgotten? This was tick season in the north woods, and any warm-blooded creature walking beneath the newly leafing trees was destined to be bombarded by the small spiderlike insects in search of a meal.

He glanced at the bug crawling up the sleeve of Pippi's sweater. Was there any way to break it to her gently? He cleared his throat. "That appears to be a member of the super-family Ixodoidea, of the order Acarina."

"Commonly known as?" Her voice was faint.

"Um, a wood tick."

Her shrill scream rent the dreaming stillness of the woods and open fields. She dropped everything she was carrying and ran for open ground, making frantic motions with her arms as she tried to brush away the ticks.

Jeremy flung his burden to the ground and leaped after her. He caught her in his arms just as she stumbled in the boulder-strewn field.

"It's all right, love. It's all right," he crooned softly, holding her against him as his hands glided gently but firmly over her body, dislodging any ticks that remained.

The sound of her gasping, frightened sobs tore at his heart. "Hush, Pip. I won't let them hurt you." He carefully threaded his fingers through her bright, soft hair and massaged every inch of her scalp with his fingertips. "None in your hair," he reported. Pippi shuddered.

His fingers moved on to make a minute inspection of her neck, reaching down under the collar of her cotton shirt for a brief check of her upper back and shoulders. He was ashamed of the instant ache of desire he felt as his hands slid over her smooth, bare skin. Dammit, the last thing she needed from him right now was lust! The terrified quivering of her body told him that.

"I think we got them off you in time," he said gently, dropping his hands to his sides.

She loosed a quavery sigh. "Before they settled down to suck my blood, you mean?" Her face was faintly flushed and her lashes were still spiked with tears. Jeremy fought the urge to pull her trembling body back into his arms.

"Yup. Long before that." He quirked his mouth in what he hoped was a reassuring smile, and handed her his handkerchief.

"This handkerchief sure looks familiar." She laughed shakily. After wiping her eyes she took a deep breath and then exhaled with such force that it fluttered the curls on her forehead. "Sorry I acted so dumb just now. But ticks scare me silly."

"So I noticed." His ironic understatement

caused her to flick her small red tongue out at him, and the sight was so distracting that Jeremy almost forgot what he was going to say next.

"Um . . . you don't owe me any apologies, Pip. You had every right to be scared. Ticks are nasty little parasites, and they can cause serious infections. *I'm* the one who should apologize for bringing you here at this time of year."

"You didn't know I'd freak out like that. In fact, *I* didn't know I'd freak out like that!" She sighed gloomily and sank down onto a nearby outcropping of rock. "This makes one more hang-up to add to my list. All these years I've thought of myself as a reasonably sane, mentally well-balanced person. But now I find out I'm slightly cuckoo!"

He laughed indulgently and squatted down next to her. "I've got news for you, Pip. The whole world is slightly cuckoo. It's nothing to worry about."

"But I *am* worried! First it was just fear of heights, but now I've also got a wood-tick phobia! And that's not all! My mother is convinced I have a predilection for men who are just like my father, which sounds pretty darn kinky to me! And, to top it off, I've been talking to myself out loud lately. Isn't that supposed to be a sign of mental instability?"

Jeremy blinked. "Your mother is convinced of *what*?"

"She says all the men I've ever thought I was in love with have reminded her of my father," she confessed shamefacedly. "But it doesn't make any sense! I haven't seen the guy since I was four years old! Why should he have any influence over the choices I've made?"

She looked so bewildered and indignant that Jeremy instinctively reached out to her, taking her hand and squeezing it gently into the warmth of his palm. His brain reacted to her revelation as if a light had been switched on in a pitch-dark room. Suddenly, so many things were clear to him.

"Could it have something to do with that little girl you told me was still hidden inside of you?" he asked with barely contained excitement. "You know—the one who still blames herself because her father went away?"

"I suppose," she said doubtfully. "But . . ." She shrugged helplessly, and Jeremy found himself slipping his arm around her shoulders.

"Maybe," he mused, "what you thought was love was just a confused little girl's attempt to re-create a relationship like the one with your father. You wanted a second chance at keeping what you'd once lost, at succeeding where you felt you'd once failed."

"Maybe." Her sigh sent vibrations through every nerve and muscle in his arm. "But it seems so pathetic! I'm supposed to be a grown woman, dammit! I can't spend the rest of my life trying to change something that happened when I was only four years old."

"Of course not. And there's no reason to keep repeating the mistakes of the past now that you realize why you made them. It's time to put it all behind you and concentrate on the future, Pip."

Her eyes rose to his in a startled, intense flash of blue before she lowered her lashes, veiling the mysterious thoughts that he longed to decipher.

"The future," she echoed softly, and her lips curved in an enigmatic smile. "You'd be surprised how much I've been concentrating on that lately."

"That's good," he said, wondering at the trace of hidden meaning in her voice.

He wanted to ask if Marc was part of the past she was ready to put behind her. And was he, Jeremy, part of the future she was ready to embrace? Literally embrace, perhaps? Lord, he hoped so!

But he knew it was too soon. He mustn't push her. He'd done that the night before, with mixed results. Now was the time for patience. She needed a chance to adjust to the idea that they could be lovers. It had to be her choice as well as his.

He stood up abruptly. All his good intentions would vanish like smoke in the wind if he sat there much longer with his arm around Pippi's soft, slim, curved body.

She was so warm and vital and glowing with life that holding her was like cupping a flame in the palms of his hands. If he wasn't careful, that flame would ignite his flesh like dry tinder.

And that might be his biggest mistake of all. Maybe this weekend was a crazy risk—too much temptation for his already precarious self-control. He was going to have to guard himself like a jailer watching over Harry Houdini! Otherwise he might end up ruining everything by giving in too soon to his own overpowering desires.

"Shall we make a run for the cabin?" he suggested. "Don't forget, there's still the present to concentrate on. Wood ticks and all," he added wryly.

"I'm ready to concentrate on that too," she assured him, and for an instant he thought he saw a faint, suggestive twinkle in her eye. "Wood ticks and *all*."

Pippi was worried.

How was she going to seduce Jeremy if he didn't give her the least bit of encouragement? He was acting as if the scene on his deck had never happened.

She sighed and took another sip of wine, glancing over to where he sat in a rustic, handmade chair with his feet propped up on a padded orange crate. He wasn't lifting a finger to take advantage of the warm, cozy, romantic atmosphere in the cabin. Damn. Her body practically burst into flame every time he came near her, but the fever didn't seem to be catching. Or else he was immune today.

The tick incident was a perfect example. Even in the midst of downright hysteria, her body had responded instantly to Jeremy's touch, trembling with the sweet, tormenting ache of her desire for him. But *he* had run his hands over her, searching for ticks, with no more reaction than if she had been a department store mannikin!

This evening *could* have been the perfect occasion for romance, she thought. They'd eaten outdoors, under an old beach umbrella that Jeremy had set up to protect them from dropping ticks. The steaks, grilled over an open fire, were delicious. The view of the sunset through the pines had been breathtaking, and the low murmur of the nearby river was as soothing as soft music. When the night air grew chilly, they had moved indoors to sit by a blazing fire in the cabin's ancient stone fireplace. Oh, yes, it could have been very romantic. But Jeremy seemed determined not to let that happen.

From the way he was acting, Pippi thought miserably, you would believe she was a modern-day Medusa who would turn him to stone if he so much as looked at her. Frankly, it wasn't easy trying to seduce a man who seemed intent on ignoring you.

At the risk of being painfully obvious she had tried every trick she knew. In fact, they were the same tricks she'd taught him two weeks ago— sultry suggestive shadings in her voice, enigmatic smiles, fleeting glances, and "accidental-on-purpose" moments of physical contact.

But all to no avail. Jeremy just seemed to get quieter and more withdrawn, as if he were keeping himself locked behind impenetrable walls. Pippi was getting desperate.

Firelight flickered on the rough log walls, and the shadows drew close about their two silent figures. The door to the cabin's only bedroom yawned dark as the mouth of a cave. Soon it would be time for her to retire to the large, old-fashioned bed with the hard mattress, squeaky springs, and painted iron bedposts. She would be spending the night there, in her borrowed sleeping bag, alone. Jeremy had made it clear he intended to spread his sleeping bag out on the hard plank floor in front of the fire.

The question was, was she going to let him get away with it? The answer was no. She was too much in love with him to let this chance slip away.

"I'm going to bed," she announced, setting down her wineglass and standing up. She bit her lip, wondering if it was time to try something blatant, like "Care to come with me?" But she was too afraid Jeremy might say no.

"An early night sounds like a good idea," he said, flashing her an uneasy smile. Pippi noticed that his knuckles were turning white where he'd gripped the arms of his chair. "After all, you've had a rough day."

"Boy, have I ever!" she muttered to herself. Louder, she said, "I'll bet you have too."

"It's had its moments." There was an awkward silence while Pippi tried to gather enough courage to issue the invitation she'd been hoping he would simply read in her eyes.

"If—"

"I—"

They'd both spoken at once. Now they both broke into nervous laughter.

"You go first," Jeremy said.

"No, *you* go first. Please," Pippi insisted.

"I just wanted to let you know that I managed to get the wood stove in the kitchen going, so there should be some hot water if you'd like to wash up."

"Oh, thanks." Oh, damn. She'd been hoping he was about to say something a bit more personal than *that*.

"And what were *you* going to say, Pip?"

"Omigosh, I've forgotten!" she lied. It had suddenly occurred to her what she must look like after her trials and tribulations of this afternoon. The nearest mirror was back in the car, but she didn't need a mirror to tell her that her hair was a mess, and no doubt her face was streaked with mud. No wonder Jeremy wasn't succumbing to her wiles. Who'd ever heard of a temptress with a dirty face?

"I think I will wash up now," she said. "I must look a sight."

"You look fine," he said, but she knew he was only being polite. "Fine" was not how she wanted to look to Jeremy tonight. Alluring, irresistible, and sexy were more like it.

She carried the brown paper sack containing her soap, towel, sponge, toothbrush, and nightie out to the kitchen, which was a small, added-on room housing a large cast-iron stove and a table and chairs. Whoever built the kitchen obviously hadn't realized the importance of counter space, Pippi noted.

After a trip outside to the little shed that did not boast a half moon over its door, she undressed in the kitchen and gave herself a hasty sponge bath.

No matter how hard she scrubbed, she still

smelled of the insect repellent she'd earlier splashed on so lavishly at Jeremy's insistence. He'd thought it might keep the ticks away, even though it was meant for mosquitoes. And to think that she'd actually worried about what fragrance to wear tonight! Little had she known she'd be reeking of "eau de Cutter."

She smoothed on scented body lotion, then lifted her arms to slip into the whisper-soft silk night-shirt. Its classic simplicity complemented the sleek lines of her legs and arms, and emphasized the gentle curves of her hips and breasts.

Sitting on a kitchen chair, she carefully combed out all the tangles in her hair. When she was finished, her curls were like a rich, flaming aureole, radiant above the stark white of her nightshirt.

Taking a deep breath to calm the fluttering in her stomach, she stood up and tiptoed, barefoot, across the kitchen floor. She paused in the door-way to the cabin's main room. As her pale, shimmering figure caught the glow of the firelight, Jeremy glanced up.

Never had Pippi been so conscious of her own vulnerable, pliant nakedness beneath the garment she was wearing. From clear across the room she heard Jeremy's sharp intake of breath when he saw her. For an unforgettable instant his eyes blazed with passionate, powerful hunger, and her senses reeled in response. But almost immediately his eyelids hooded the telltale flare of emotion.

"Jeremy?" she said softly. He must want her. He must! But why was he so determined to fight it?

"Yes?" His voice was low and wary, but she thought she detected a betraying note of breathlessness.

She left the shelter of the doorway and walked toward the taut, still man reclining by the fireplace. The hem of her silk nightshirt swished teasingly against her bare thighs. Jeremy's jaw was clenched so hard that she could see small knots of muscle stand out in his cheeks. She almost lost her nerve, but kept walking forward.

Her thoughts and her pulse raced furiously. What was she going to say to him? How was she going to pull this off if he didn't give her a little help? Should she just give up right now and crawl headfirst into her sleeping bag to cry herself to sleep?

She sank down onto her knees beside his chair. "Can I ask you a favor?" she heard herself inquire in a tremulous voice.

He shrugged and his confused brown eyes were trained on a spot just to the left of her face. "Sure," he said gruffly.

"Won't you please . . . check to make sure I don't have any more ticks on me?" she said, shuddering delicately.

"Pip, I'm not sure that's—"

"Please!" she begged, blushing hotly at her own outrageous duplicity. "I keep thinking I feel an itch. Maybe it's all in my mind, but I'll never get to sleep if I keep imagining one of *them* is on me!"

At least that wasn't a complete fabrication—she *did* feel an "itch." But she knew darn well it had nothing to do with ticks.

"Okay." His voice was slightly hoarse. He lowered his legs off the footstool, planted his feet on the floor, and sat up straight before reaching an unsteady hand out to her. "Shall I check your scalp first?"

"Mmm."

The slow caress of his fingers over the sensitive skin along her hairline was a subtle enchantment. "That feels so good," she murmured, rubbing her temple against his palm in a catlike gesture of affectionate pleasure-seeking.

His hand stilled. "Pip?"

"Found any ticks yet?" she asked hastily.

"Not yet." The look in his eyes was one of such fierce, enthralled concentration that Pippi felt hot and breathless and transparent beneath his gaze. His fingers moved on, weaving an intricate pattern of countless minute sensations over every inch of her scalp. The cumulative effect was utterly marvelous.

"I think you've just discovered a new erogenous zone," she muttered under her breath as the stirrings of response flickered throughout her whole body.

"Did you say something, Pip?"

"Who, me? No."

His fingers fanned through her hair, combing out each sleek, curling strand from root to tip. "Definitely no ticks there," he said at last.

She gave a sigh she hoped he would interpret as one of relief. "But I still feel an itch," she whispered huskily.

This time it was Jeremy who muttered an inaudible comment. He took a deep, shaky breath and asked, "Where?"

She carefully kept her face innocent of all expression as she answered him, but she couldn't quite hide the teasing sparkle in her bright eyes. "Well, there's a sort of quivery feeling along my spine, for starters."

He went absolutely still. Pippi watched as the pupils of his eyes narrowed to tiny pinpricks of darkness and then flared wide into dark pools of unfathomable emotion.

"For *starters*, Pip?" A hesitant, questioning smile tugged at the corners of his mouth.

"That's what I said, Holt." She answered his smile and held her breath, waiting for his reaction.

"Then I'd better check you *very* carefully, hadn't I?" he murmured throatily as his hands closed over her shoulders. "We can't let a single itch go unexamined. Come closer."

She eagerly followed the urging of his hands until she was kneeling between his thighs, resting her palms on their muscled hardness for support as she gazed up into his face.

"Where did you say that quivery feeling was— your spine?" he asked. She nodded and closed her eyes as his fingertips stroked their way down her back, exploring every link of her vertebrae through the gossamer-soft silk.

When his hands reached the small of her back, she opened her eyes wide in seeming alarm. "Are you *sure* it's enough to just feel for ticks through my nightgown?" she asked. "What if you missed one? Maybe you'd better check . . . underneath, just in case."

"You can't be too careful," he agreed, deadpan.

His palms skimmed down the slick fabric that covered her soft curves, pausing at the hem before sliding underneath and upward. While his hands intimately kneaded the smooth, bare flesh at the backs of her thighs, they also exerted a subtle foward pressure that caused her hips to arch into the hard angle of his thighs.

He groaned softly as she rubbed against the hard warmth of his maleness. "Why, Jeremy, do you feel an itch too?" she asked demurely. "Shall I check *you* for ticks?"

Without giving him time to answer, she began unbuttoning his plaid flannel shirt. When her fingers caressed the firm, muscled beauty of his naked chest, she felt a thrill of exultation. At last she could touch him freely. All his gloriously sculpted strength and grace that had tantalized her every Saturday morning for months was now warm and quivering beneath her seeking, tingling fingertips. And she no longer had to hide the way he made her feel. She didn't have to play games anymore.

"I want you, Jeremy," she whispered as he stroked the satiny, rounded curves of her bottom. *And I love you*, she thought, but wasn't quite brave enough to say the words aloud just yet.

"The feeling is one hundred percent mutual." With a sudden flexing of his powerful arm muscles he swung her up onto his lap and pulled her hard against his chest.

"There you go again with those exact numbers!" she said breathlessly. "Only an accountant would think in percentages at a moment like this!"

"Who's *thinking*?" he murmured against her neck. "Lady, there's no number in the universe that could measure the way I feel. I'm on fire for you!"

His mouth sought and clung to hers with a passionate thirsting, as if the moistness of her lips and tongue could quench the flame within him. But the melding of their mouths only stirred the blaze to burn hotter and brighter in both of them.

His fingers shook as he undid the tiny buttons down the front of her nightie. When he parted the while silk to reveal the rosy fullness her nipples and the creamy perfection of her breasts, his breath caught in his throat.

"You are so lovely." Lowering his head, he wreathed the budding tips with dewy, arousing kisses. Her fingers dug into the smooth, sleek skin of his shoulders as she felt the sweet pressure of desire building inside her.

He eased the nightshirt down off her shoulders as he took the ripe fullness of her breast into his mouth.

"Oh, yes, yes," Pippi breathed, arching more fully into his wet, erotic caress. One errant lock of Jeremy's hair fell forward, softly brushing her bare flesh, and she brought her hands up to cradle his head against her, murmuring his name over and over again.

When he drew back his head, it was only to give her a long, purposeful look before rising swiftly to his feet, carrying her up with him in his warm, strong arms. Her nightshirt slithered down her legs and drifted to the floor like a wisp of cloud. Her naked body felt feather-light as he carried her to the bedroom.

He lowered her carefully onto the sleeping bag spread out on the mattress, then sat down beside her. He fumbled for matches to light the candle stub sitting on the upended fruit crate that served as a nightstand. Within seconds the room was bathed in the soft glow of candlelight.

"Afraid of the dark?" she teased, feeling her heart beat like thunder as he turned to her.

"Not with you here to protect me." He smiled as his knuckle traced the petal-soft curve of her cheek, but then his expression grew serious. "But I do want to look at you while we make love. I want to see your face, your body, your feelings—all of you. And I want you to *know* that I'm seeing *you*, and only you. No more misunderstandings like last night."

She nodded and gave him a misty smile. He sounded so sure, so loving.

His eyes locked with hers as he stood up to shrug the shirt off his shoulders and strip down his jeans and underwear. Pippi sucked in her breath at the brief, tantalizing glimpse she had of his trim hips, his hard, muscled buttocks, at his obvious arousal. Then he stretched out beside her on the bed.

His smile was half shy, half proud as he read the fervent admiration in her gaze. "I'll bet you're thinking, 'Not bad for an accountant,' " he teased.

"Who's *thinking*?" she asked breathlessly, echoing his earlier declaration. She closed her eyes as his lips took hers with a hungry, tender power and his hands glided down the curves and hollows of her body.

When he parted her thighs, she gave a whimper of uncontainable excitement. She clung to him as his fingers moved, strumming intimately against her flesh. Their throbbing tempo was as quick as the fluttering pulse of a bird, whirling her aloft on a sharp, sudden rush of dizzying pleasure. Her body felt poised on the brink of rapturous flight.

"Are you ready for me to love you, Pip?" His hoarse, urgent whisper feathered against her ear, sending a shaft of pure emotion straight to her heart.

"Yes . . . yes . . . yes!"

"Then hold on tight, love." He lifted his body over hers. Their eyes met and merged in absolute oneness of desire as she gripped him at the waist, feeling his muscles taut and ready beneath his hot, sweat-slickened skin. A heartbeat later their loins arched together into ascending flight.

The only sounds were their panting breaths, their drumming heartbeats, and the rhythmic sighing and squeaking of the bedsprings as Jeremy glided into her again and again. His slow, controlled, stroking thrusts were like the beating of giant wings, lifting them both upward in an ever-accelerating spiral of urgency.

When the moment of release came at last, they clung together in a shimmering, soaring explosion of joy. Afterward, they rested their buoyant, weightless, boneless bodies in each other's arms, floating gradually back to a state where words were possible once more.

Ten

"Omigosh," Pippi breathed softly with reverent wonder.

"Omigosh yourself, kid." Jeremy's eyes were soft, reflecting the bright candle flame. "You take my breath away, Pip."

"I'm glad," she whispered, tenderly framing his face with her hands, brushing back his damp, silky hair. "Because that's what you do to me too."

They gazed into each other's eyes, each trying to read the thoughts and emotions that quivered on the brink of expression in the other's face.

Pippi yearned to say aloud the words that were hovering on her lips. Words of boundless love and commitment. But Jeremy hadn't asked her for those things. Come to think of it, he hadn't even asked her for *this*. She'd just more or less volunteered.

Now she must force herself to give him time. After what they'd just shared, he surely knew how she felt about him. But if she put it into words, he might feel pressured to respond before he was sure of his own feelings. And if it turned out he was still hopelessly in love with Mary, Pippi's declaration of love would only embarrass him. She didn't want that. But, oh, how she wished she knew what their lovemaking had meant to him.

But Jeremy wasn't saying much. His expression was thoughtful and intense as he watched her. Once he cleared his throat as if he were about to speak, but no words came out. When the silence had stretched between them for several minutes, he sighed.

"It's getting chilly," he said. "Why don't I get my sleeping bag and zip it together with yours?"

"I'd like that."

He returned in less than a minute with the other sleeping bag. Pippi watched his head bent in concentration as he deftly worked the zipper mechanism to link the two sleeping bags together.

His eyelashes were tipped with gold in the candlelight, and his bare shoulders and thighs were gilded in a creamy glow. Just the sight of him suffused her with a special warmth.

It occurred to her that she now knew the answer to that intriguing question she'd asked herself so long ago it seemed: Was Jeremy a shy, tender lover, or a bold, aggressive one?

The answer was, he was a complex, astonishing, irresistible blend of both. But the question hardly seemed relevant anymore. Jeremy was Jeremy, unique and incomparable. Making love with him was an experience that transcended the physical. It was a permeation of her soul and senses with the very essence of the man she loved.

He finished zipping the sleeping bags together and drew the top layer up under her chin, tucking it tight around her. "I'd better bank down the fires and close up for the night," he said, and gave her an intimate smile. "Will you save a place for me here?"

"Only if you hurry right back. And please don't bank down *all* the fires."

He laughed and leaned over to join his mouth with hers in a long, lingering kiss of ever-deepening sensuality that had her sighing with regret when he drew away. "I promise I'll hurry."

Pippi lay in bed, listening to Jeremy rake the ashes in the fireplace and adjust the dampers on the kitchen stove. A short silence followed, and she strained to hear what he was doing. Soon she recognized the thud of booted feet on the kitchen floor, followed by the slam of the cabin door.

She guessed that he had put his muddy boots on to make a visit to the little shed in back. She giggled aloud at the picture her imagination conjured up, of a stark-naked man in hiking boots.

But her giggles soon died away as she lay alone in the big bed, feeling doubts trickle in like drafts of cold air. Had she been wrong to act like a brazen hussy tonight? Nothing had ever felt so right as their lovemaking, but still . . . She had practically forced Jeremy into it. Or had she? Only last night he'd been the one seducing *her*.

"Your nose is twitching like mad," Jeremy's voice rumbled from the doorway. "What's confusing you tonight, Pip?"

She glanced up, startled, and tried to laugh.

"Tell me," he demanded gently, crossing the room and sinking down beside her on the bed, keeping his gaze on her face.

"You are." The confession was out before she had time to think it through. "You confuse me."

"How do I do that?"

"Because I can't tell what you're thinking, what

you're feeling," she burst out. Looking him square in the eyes and lifting her chin, she asked, "Are you sorry we made love just now?"

"Of course I'm not sorry!" he said. "How could I be sorry, Pip? Sorry for something as miraculous as what we shared tonight? No way."

The certainty in his voice was reassuring. Still . . . "But it's not what you wanted, is it?" she asked forlornly. "I mean, I practically *threw* myself at you! It's just like what happened before, except—"

"Hold on a minute, Pip. Now you're the one confusing *me!*" he exclaimed. "First of all, believe me, I wanted this. I wanted *you*. And I still do. But how is what happened tonight like *anything* that's ever happened before?" His face softened as he smiled reminiscently and murmured, "It certainly felt unique to me."

"True. Because last time I made a pass at you, you turned me down flat," Pippi reminded him gloomily.

"Last time *what?* What are you talking about?"

She sighed. "Think back, Jeremy. Six months ago. Rob and I had just broken up, and one night my friends kept buying me drinks to 'cheer me up.' It wasn't working. I remember I suddenly felt this crazy, overpowering need to see you, to talk to you. So my friends obligingly dropped me off at your house. I was totally plastered, obviously."

"It *was* rather obvious," Jeremy said with that wryly affectionate grin of his that she knew and loved so well.

She blushed. "So you do remember."

"I remember that you were upset, crying. I held you in my arms to comfort you, and then I took you home."

"There was more to it than that, Jeremy."

"Yes." He drew a long, deep breath. "There was

more. You said, 'Stay with me.' " He lowered his head next to hers on the pillow so their faces were almost touching. "Until now I wasn't sure you even remembered."

"So why didn't you?" she asked in a thick, tremulous voice. "Why didn't you stay with me that night? Was it because of Mary?"

"No."

"Then why?"

"Because I'm not the kind of guy who takes advantage of my friends when they're upset and . . . inebriated. Not even when I'm very, very tempted."

"Were you? Tempted, I mean?"

He nodded, and she was amazed to see a slight flush creep over his face.

"It wouldn't have been taking advantage," she said, lowering her lashes.

"Yes, it would've." He sighed. "You're my best friend, Pip. And what kind of friend would I be if you couldn't count on me to keep you from making a reckless, impulsive decision you might regret once you were sober again?"

"Regret?" She laughed huskily. "Making love with you isn't the kind of experience I could ever regret, Jeremy."

"Me neither." Though he chuckled softly, his eyes betrayed the intensity of his emotion. His hand sought hers inside the sleeping bag and he drew it to his face, pressing his lips against her palm. "If only I'd guessed, six months ago . . ."

But that thought brought him smack up against a few hard, unpleasant facts he'd been forgetting. His hand clenched on Pippi's, and he frowned.

"But how *could* I have guessed?" he asked almost angrily. "At the time it wasn't even clear that your breakup with Rob would turn out to be permanent. After all, you'd made up with him a dozen times before."

Jeremy's abrupt shift of mood caught Pippi by surprise. She felt so vulnerable, almost fragile, after their physical intimacy, that his harsh tone cut like the lash of a whip. But there was worse to come.

"In fact, you couldn't have been serious about wanting me six months ago." His voice was so hard that she felt bruised by the sound. "Only a few days after inviting me to share your bed, you informed me you were madly in love with Marc!"

She gave an agonized whimper of protest. But how could she blame him for condemning her? He saw only the mistakes she'd made. What he didn't see were the painful, confusing emotions that had been in her heart at the time, blinding her.

She now knew that when she'd instinctively reached out to Jeremy for comfort six months earlier, it was because she was already half in love with him without even realizing it. That was why his seeming rejection had cut her so deeply.

She'd still been reeling from the hurt and humiliation of it when she first met Marc. And she'd also had deep-rooted feelings of guilt and failure over the broken relationship with Rob. Every time she failed at love it brought back all the childhood trauma of her father's desertion.

No wonder it had been so easy to misjudge the nature of her feelings for Marc! Like a shipwreck victim clinging to a piece of wreckage, she had seized the new chance he seemed to offer. She'd been determined to make the relationship succeed. But of course it had turned out to be a ghastly mistake.

"I thought I loved him," she told Jeremy. "But it

was all a mistake. In fact, there's something you should know. Marc and I have split up."

If she had hoped this knowledge might soften Jeremy's attitude, she soon learned her mistake.

"The hell you have!" He abruptly rolled away from her and sat up on the edge of the bed. His head was bowed so that all Pippi could see of him was the hard, rigid line of his back. "When did this happen?"

"R-recently." The note of contempt in his voice kept her from saying more.

He turned toward her with a bitter smile. "So this is just like what happened six months ago, isn't it? Except now you're on the rebound from Marc instead of from Rob. And this time *I'm* the poor slob who's going to get written off as just another of your 'mistakes.' "

"No! That's not true!" All in the same breath she found herself blurting out what she'd been holding in for so long. "Jeremy, I love you!"

"Oh, Pip." He looked as if he wanted to cry, but instead he broke into mirthless, hollow laughter. "I've waited so long to hear those words, but I never dreamed they would leave me feeling so . . . cynical. So empty."

She stared at him, uncomprehending.

"You're *always* sure you're in love, Pip. At the time. It's only later that you realize it was all a mistake."

"But this time is dif—"

"Different," he interrupted. "Sure it is. But you say *that* every time too."

She understood then the diabolical trap she'd set for herself. Like the boy who cried "wolf," she'd cried "love" too many times to be taken seriously now that the real thing had come along at last. Nothing she could say would convince Jeremy that her love was genuine. And yet she knew beyond all doubt that what she felt for him was unique and real and deep and true. There could be no mistake.

Jeremy stood up and started pulling his clothes back on.

"Where are you going?" she asked as he stepped into his pants.

"To sit and think for a while." He zipped up his jeans.

She swallowed her pride. "Will you be coming back . . . to bed?"

"I don't think so, Pip." He picked up his shirt.

"Oh." Hot tears pressed against her lids, but she refused to let them fall. "You'd better take your sleeping bag, then, or you'll be cold." She sat up and reached blindly for the tab of the zipper that joined their bags together.

His hand closed over hers. "Let me," he said. His touch felt like fire against her skin, and her whole body jerked with the shock of it.

In that instant her dammed-up tears escaped and went spilling down her cheeks, cascading from her face to her naked breasts. She heard the harsh rasp of Jeremy's indrawn breath even as she looked up and saw the torment and desire in his eyes.

The flannel shirt slipped from his grasp and fell to the floor. "Oh, Pip," he groaned, and then his lips were moving swiftly, sweetly, over her tear-drenched flesh. Her eyelids, her cheeks, her trembling mouth, and her soft, swollen-tipped breasts felt the hot, arousing caress of his lips and tongue.

Pippi didn't pause to ask herself if Jeremy was experiencing a true change of heart or was merely giving in to overpowering sexual desire. At the moment it didn't seem to matter.

Heat flashed along her limbs like a sheet of

scorching flame as he stretched out along the length of her and pressed her shoulders back against the bed. Through the down thickness of the sleeping bag she could feel the unyielding pressure of his thighs, while his tongue filled her breathless mouth with a throbbing ache of desire.

In feverish delight she ran her palms down the satiny skin of his bare back, feeling the shifting pattern of contracting muscle, savoring the hard symmetry of his ribs. Her fingers slid beneath the coarse denim at his waist to explore the velvety texture of his buttocks.

Soon, he was tugging at the sleeping bag zipper, then shifting his weight so he could uncover her flushed, bare body. Meanwhile, she was busy with some tugging and unzipping of her own as she pulled off his jeans.

Their bodies came together, bathed in a sheen of perspiration that bonded his flesh to hers, heightening the sweet sensations of touching and being touched. Their mouths merged and trembled in the depths of a kiss that burned with unutterable emotion.

Jeremy's hands were shaking as they made a slow, sliding journey up the muscled curves of Pippi's thighs, seeking the heart of her body's ferment. Her slim legs shifted and wound themselves round him, pressing him closer.

"Come inside," she whispered urgently, and he did. As she gathered him into her and they began to rock and glide in the ancient rhythm of love, she knew that no matter what tomorrow might bring, at least for tonight she could call this man her own. As she was his. Completely.

"Wake up, Pip! We've got to get the hell out of here!"

Groggily, Pippi stirred in the sleeping bag and opened one bleary eye to blink at the bearer of these urgent, unwelcome, and incomprehensible tidings. What was Jeremy doing out of bed?

"Get up!" he urged.

"What?" she groaned.

"There's a doozy of a storm heading this way. The road is muddy enough now, but an inch or two of rain could turn it into a quagmire. We've got to leave right this minute, before we get stuck here indefinitely."

"But it's pitch dark out! It must be the middle of the night," she complained, glancing out the window.

"The sun came up an hour ago. You just can't see it right now because of all the thunderheads. Will you *hurry*?"

She climbed out of bed and rummaged around, looking for her clean underwear. "Is there any coffee?"

"We don't have time for coffee. Besides, I've already doused all the fires. Let's get going."

Well. So much for any lingering, romantic afterglow from their lovemaking the night before! Pippi thought.

Five minutes later she was slogging down the track toward the car, feeling absolutely rock-bottom miserable. Her feet hurt, her hair needed combing, her stomach was growling ferociously, and she would have traded anything she owned for just one cup of hot coffee.

The wind whipped by in fitful gusts, tossing the tree branches and scouring the grass. It was cold and the sky was black with storm clouds. She shivered. All this, and ticks too—though none of those had landed on her so far today, thank goodness!

She would have felt much more cheerful if

Jeremy had bothered to smile, but he looked as grim and ominous as the thunderclouds. Obviously, he couldn't *wait* to get out of there. Heaven forbid that he should get stranded alone at the cabin with *her*! That clearly wasn't his idea of a good time. Pippi sighed.

She wondered whether he'd lain awake after the sweet, desperate fire of their lovemaking had been spent. She herself had drifted swiftly into sleep, reassured by the rhythmic caress of his hand on her hair, the smooth warmth of his shoulder beneath her cheek, and the steady thudding of his heartbeat near her ear. But what thoughts had he been thinking while she slept?

Her conjectures were cut short as the first, scattered icy raindrops came pelting down. "Run!" Jeremy commanded, and they both raced the last few yards to the car.

"Oh," Pippi groaned as she sank into the passenger seat, "I'm getting blisters on my blisters."

Jeremy started the car and carefully began reversing along the track, backing slowly enough to control the steering, but fast enough to maintain their momentum so they wouldn't get stuck. His task wasn't made any easier by the pellets of rain that plastered the rear window, forcing him to stick his head out the side window to see where he was going.

Pippi breathed a sigh of relief and removed her chewed-upon knuckles from her mouth when the tires finally backed onto solid pavement. Jeremy grinned as he drew his dripping head back into the car and rolled up the window.

"Thank heavens we didn't have to get out and push!" he said. "I've had about all the disasters I can take in one weekend."

Indeed. Pippi felt his words like a slap in the face.

Was that all it had been to him, then—a series of disasters? And did he count being seduced into her bed as one of those disasters? The biggest one of all, perhaps?

The thought was thoroughly demoralizing. For the first time, Pippi faced her own defeat. She'd lost her gamble. Jeremy didn't love her, and he never would. All her love, and all her loving, hadn't been enough to win his heart. He thought she was shallow and fickle and emotionally unstable.

Her tiny, choking sob went unheard amid the tumult of the storm. Rain lashed the windshield and blew in sheets across the road. The wind tugged at the car, and only Jeremy's firm grip on the wheel kept them on the pavement. His attention was riveted on the watery ribbon of highway ahead as he strained to see what lay beyond the heavy curtain of rain.

"We'll stop for breakfast at the first place we see, okay?" he suggested, not taking his eyes off the road.

"Okay." Somehow she managed to make her voice sound normal.

Several minutes farther on they pulled into the parking lot of a roadside café. The warmth and brightness inside were a welcome contrast to the storm raging outside. The waitress kept up a flow of chatter about the weather as she poured coffee for them and took their orders.

Pippi took several gulps of coffee and then excused herself to go to the ladies' room. Once she had washed her face, combed her hair, and applied a touch of makeup, she felt a bit better. But not much.

Her heart sank as she faced Jeremy's serious, intense face across the table. His hair was still dark and wet with rain, and his eyes were bright and keen despite the lines of weariness around them.

"We have to talk, Pip."

She choked and sputtered on a mouthful of coffee. "Oh?"

"I guess you realize this weekend didn't go quite the way I'd planned. And I don't mean just the weather."

She managed to nod, but she felt a queasy, panicky sensation at the pit of her stomach. She didn't want to hear this. She didn't have the strength. If she had to look Jeremy in the face while he tried to break it to her gently that their making love had been a mistake that wouldn't be repeated, she would break down and make a fool of herself.

"I hadn't foreseen," he said, "that you and I would become lovers so quickly, before we reached a . . . a clearer understanding of our feelings for each other. It took me by surprise, and I'm afraid. . . ." He hesitated, flushing with chagrin. "I'm afraid, in the heat of the moment last night, I said some things that—"

"I understand," she broke in crisply. Her jaw muscles ached with the strain of hiding the anguish she felt. Last night he'd said that she took his breath away, that what they'd shared was "miraculous," and that he could never be sorry it had happened. Now he'd changed his mind. It was as simple as that.

"You understand? But how can you? I haven't even explained yet. You see—"

He stopped abruptly when the waitress appeared with their order. "Ham and eggs and hash browns," she announced, setting one plate in front of Jeremy. "Your toast will be along in a minute, sir. And here's your blueberry pancakes, ma'am."

"Thank you," Pippi murmured, feeling almost

faint with relief at the interruption. But all too soon the ordeal continued.

"Pip, about last night. I'm sorry I—"

"Please, Jeremy!" she broke in. "There's no need to—"

"Here's your toast, sir," the waitress interjected.

"May I have some more coffee, please?" Pippi hastily requested, drawing an impatient frown from Jeremy.

He clamped his jaw shut in frustration while the waitress topped off Pippi's coffee cup. He took a deep breath when the waitress had bustled out of earshot.

"Maybe the stupid things I said last night aren't as important as the things I left *unsaid*." He looked very grave. "There's something I should have told you."

"Jeremy, there's no point to all these post-mortems about last night!" Pippi exclaimed in desperation. She tried to laugh. "Surely two people can spend a few hours in bed together without having to discuss and analyze and *explain* it to death the next morning!"

He looked as stunned as if she'd just punched him in the mouth and knocked out a few teeth in the process.

"But what about . . . feelings? Don't they matter? Last night you said—"

"Never mind what I said. We both said things we didn't mean. Now let's just not say anything. *Please.*"

There was a moment of grim, shocked silence. Jeremy's face went pale and hard as marble. "If that's how you feel, then you needn't worry. I've got nothing to say to you."

Eleven

Neither of them said a word to the other during all the miles between breakfast and the moment they took the freeway exit to Pippi's place.

By then Pippi knew that she'd behaved like a cowardly, childish idiot. She should have let Jeremy say whatever he thought he had to say. It couldn't have been any worse than this terrible, angry silence. Just knowing that everything was over between them hurt so much that hearing it from his own lips couldn't possibly have added to the pain. And if only she had let him tell her, she wouldn't have so many unanswered questions to torment herself with.

Finally, when it seemed likely that in five minutes they might say good-bye forever, one of those questions just popped out. "Are you still in love with Mary?" she asked.

"Huh?"

"Well, are you?"

"There's not much point in loving a woman

who's never going to love me back," he said bitterly.

"And yet you still do," Pippi concluded softly, recognizing the sad truth behind his anger. She'd never had any chance with him at all. "I'm sorry," she said.

"Don't be. It's only a matter of time till I'm over her. I can't spend the rest of my life knocking my head against a brick wall, Pip."

"Of course not." Only a matter of time. She wondered how long it would take her to get over Jeremy. Probably forever.

They turned onto her street. The sun was shining and most of the clouds were gone, but evidence of the recent storm was everywhere. Fallen tree branches lay strewn about, flower beds were in shambles, storm drains were overflowing, and wet sidewalks were steaming in the hot sun. The air smelled of damp earth.

Jeremy helped her carry her luggage up to the apartment. "I'll be in touch," he said. "Let me know if you change your mind."

"About what?" But he didn't hear her question, because he'd already turned and sprinted down the stairs.

Alone in her apartment, Pippi had plenty of depressing topics to think about. Jeremy, Jeremy, and Jeremy. He'd been *using* her this weekend, she decided angrily. Using her to try to get over his love for Mary. Damn. Too bad it hadn't worked.

But it hadn't, just the way all their plans to make Mary fall for Jeremy hadn't worked . . . on Mary. They'd worked *too* well on Pippi. Love was a funny business. What had made her think *she* was equipped to give advice on the subject?

Lord knows, Jeremy might have been better off

without her help. Could she honestly say that her own feelings hadn't interfered with giving him the best advice on how to court another woman? There were times, she realized now, when she'd held him back just when he should have gone ahead with the direct approach.

That thought gave her conscience a nasty jolt. And then her conscience gave *her* a nasty jolt. "No! I won't do it!" she protested aloud.

"But you owe it to him," her conscience reproached her. "After all, if he hadn't listened to *you*, he and Mary might have gotten together by now."

"But I don't *want* them to get together. And I'm not cut out to be a martyr!"

Unfortunately, her conscience held the trump card. "If you really loved Jeremy, you'd want him to be happy. Just because you can't have him is no reason *he* has to be miserable."

Pippi muttered an indelicate retort and stormed out of her apartment. "This is the last time I listen to *you*," she muttered as she limped down the stairs. "You might at least have given me a chance to change my shoes."

There was still some mild flooding in the streets as she drove to Jeremy's house. She thought of the muddy track to the cabin. It must be an impenetrable swamp by now. They could have been trapped there for days—without anything to eat.

She saw Jeremy the minute she turned into his driveway. He was hard to miss. Clad only in a pair of cut-off jeans and wielding a power saw, he was standing on the roof of his house. A large tree limb, still partially attached to the trunk of the towering oak that grew at the front corner of the house, had come down on the roof. Luckily, damage to the house appeared slight.

Intent on the clean-up job he had to do, he didn't see her until she hailed him from the foot of the ladder. At the sound of her voice his whole body stiffened and then, with a conscious effort, relaxed. As if in slow motion, his head swung around to face her. His expression was one of controlled inscrutability.

"I need to talk to you, Jeremy."

"Oh?" He sounded wary but not unresponsive.

"It's about Mary."

"Oh." He turned back to the tree limb. "I'm rather busy. As you can see." The taut, tapering, sexy line of his back was eloquent in its rejection of her presence.

Pippi felt a spurt of irritation. Darn it all, she was trying to help him! He could at least have the courtesy to listen. She put her foot on the bottom rung of the ladder.

"I've thought of something more you should try before you give up on her completely," she called up to him.

"Too late." His voice was so harsh, it started a shiver along Pippi's spine. "I've *already* completely given up on her. And I find it damn peculiar that you should still be promoting my relationship with Mary after what happened between you and me in bed last night!"

Pippi swallowed. No doubt it was peculiar. In her opinion it was downright stupid. But it was something she knew she had to do.

"I'm still your friend, Jeremy," she said, moving several rungs higher on the ladder in an effort to bridge the gap between them. "And I want you to be happy."

He bit off a muffled expletive. "Just take your

damn friendship and go home, Pip," he said wearily.

"But—"

Her protest was obliterated by the deafening rasp of the power saw as he switched it on and proceeded to lop several branches off the fallen tree limb.

"Jeremy Holt, you turn that thing off and listen to what I have to say!" Shouting to be heard over the loud buzzing and whining of the saw, Pippi scrambled almost to the top of the ladder. Her red head poked indignantly over the roof's edge.

Jeremy cut the motor on the saw and glared at her. "Well?"

She felt an urge to grab him by those beautiful broad shoulders of his and shake some sense into him. "I won't let you give up on Mary till you've at least told her how you feel. In all this time, it's the one thing you've never tried."

His laughter sounded nasty. There was no other way to describe it. "But I *have* tried," he said. "The trouble is, she doesn't want to listen. Besides . . ." He leveled a mocking look at her. "Weren't you the one who warned me that an outright declaration of love would be 'fatal'?"

She blushed. "That was then. This is now."

"And what makes now so different?"

"Now you've tried everything else, so you've got nothing to lose by the direct approach. In fact, maybe . . . maybe I should have suggested you try it sooner," she confessed shamefacedly.

"I don't see what difference it would have made."

"It would have made a difference to the way I feel right now, which is horribly guilty."

"Guilty?" He seemed quite taken aback. "Why?"

"Omigosh, isn't it obvious, after last night? I've been falling deeper and deeper in love with you ever since this whole thing started, and surely that must've affected the kind of advice I was giving you. Even if I didn't realize it at the time," she added ruefully.

Very carefully, Jeremy set down the power saw where it wasn't likely to go sliding down the gentle slope of the roof. Surefooted as a mountain goat, he moved across the roof to the ladder.

Before she could utter even one squeak of alarm, he grabbed her by the wrists and pulled her up beside him. Just like that. One quick tug of his powerful arms and there she was, sitting on the roof.

"Omigosh, I'm on the roof!" She glanced down between her feet and felt dizzy.

His deep, husky voice, close to her ear, sounded amused but slightly breathless. "Isn't that where you said you did your best matchmaking?"

"Only if I fall off." She squeezed her eyes tightly shut. "And I'd really rather not."

"I won't let you fall, Pip." It was true. His warm, bare, muscled arm had wrapped tightly around her. It felt so good, she convinced herself to open her eyes, and promptly felt dizzy again. Not from looking at the ground, but because Jeremy's brown eyes were only inches away, and they were so full of tender radiance that she felt she would drown in their engulfing light.

"Omigosh," she repeated.

"We've got to talk, Pip."

"Haven't I just been trying to tell you that? Of course we need to talk!" Her voice faltered a bit as she added, "About you and Mary."

"No. About *you*. And me. And Mary." He hesitated. "Last night you said you loved me. Do you still feel that way?"

She bit her lip and looked away. "I'm afraid so,"

she admitted in a faint voice. "But you mustn't worry about *me*," she insisted. "I'll get over it. You should concentrate on Mary."

"Later. First I want to know, how long have you . . . felt this way about me?"

She hung her head. "Months, I guess. At least since that night I—um—you know."

"*What*? Since *then*?" He sounded absolutely horrified.

"I didn't know it at the time, of course!" she hastened to say. "It was only after you started practicing all your romancing on me and then took me up for that glider ride that I finally realized the truth. Until then it all happened so gradually. Loving you as a friend, I never noticed my love was changing to something more."

"I see." His voice sounded strange. "Well, Pip, I'll tell you one thing. You've got no reason to feel guilty about the advice you've been giving me, because a man couldn't ask for better advice. In fact, your advice is so good that I've decided to follow it again this time."

She felt an odd pain in her chest. "Does that mean you'll be talking to Mary?"

He smiled. "I'm going to tell the woman I love exactly how I feel about her!"

"You've made the right decision, Jeremy. I'm sure you won't regret it." Too bad that wasn't true in her own case—she was already regretting it! Knowing she'd done the right thing seemed small consolation for the gnawing ache in her heart.

"There's just one thing, Pip."

"Mmm?" She was terribly afraid she might burst into tears any second now. She tugged at his hand on her shoulder, trying to free herself from the snug hold of his arm. But his arm wasn't budging.

"*How* should I tell her? Do you have any suggestions for me?"

She simply stared at him. He had done some pretty insensitive things lately, but this really took the cake. How could it not occur to him that his request was bound to be painful and embarrassing to her? The last thing she wanted right now was to offer him instructions on how to declare his love for another woman.

"Just *tell* her, for crying out loud! The simple words *I love you* should suffice." Gritting her teeth, she tried to scoot on her rear end toward the top of the ladder. Moving closer to the edge of the roof brought on a wave of dizziness, but she wanted out of the conversation so badly, she didn't even care.

"Whoa, there." Jeremy's other arm casually draped itself around her waist, exerting just enough pressure to keep her next to him. "Let's see if I've got this straight," he said, and his voice was husky and rich and vibrant with emotion.

His lips almost touched her ear as he whispered, "I love you."

A spasm of pain went through every clenched muscle in Pippi's body. "You've got it straight," she said grimly.

He took her by the shoulders and lowered her gently onto the rough shingles of the roof. His muscled thighs straddled her hips as he knelt above her. His lips were smiling and his brown eyes were glowing.

"Pip, I love you."

She blinked back furious, bitter tears and glared up at him. "Listen, you insensitive clod! If you don't stop practicing on me, I'm going to shove you right off this roof!"

"But I'm not practicing."

Through the blur of her unshed tears, she saw his face moving closer. "Then what the hell *are* you doing?" she demanded in a desperate voice as he nuzzled the delicate skin of her throat.

"Isn't it obvious?" His eyes were warm and twinkling and tender with emotion. "I'm trying to tell you that I love you, Pip."

Her jaw dropped open. She felt an explosion inside her chest. Love, joy, fear, shock, and disbelief all rushed together in an overwhelming jumble.

"But you love Mary," she said.

"No. I love *you*."

And suddenly, she believed him. *He loved her!* "Omigosh! Jeremy! You love me!"

The wonder of it was so great that she just lay there staring up at him with a silly grin on her face for a whole five seconds before she came to her senses and flung her arms around his neck with a tiny sob of gladness. Excitement and jubilation flooded through her like intoxicants invading her bloodstream. The sunlight shimmered on Jeremy's smooth bare shoulders and glinted golden in his light brown hair as he bent his head to kiss her.

Their mouths met and joined in wordless communion. Their lips and tongues conveyed feelings too urgent to be translated into a spoken language. Each throbbing touch was like a pebble dropped into a pool, triggering infinite rippling circles of meaning and sensation.

When they broke apart for air, Pippi felt as if she were melting against the sun-warmed shingles of the roof. She lay there, panting, stunned by the sudden richness and rightness of it all.

"How long have you known?" she asked shyly. She felt like a child exploring a marvelous, magical toy store. Her brain was busy with intriguing speculations. Was it last night? On his deck the night before that? The day they went soaring? The night they went dancing? *When?*

The silence wore on so long that she wrinkled her nose and eyed Jeremy more closely. Uh-oh. He had an apprehensive look on his face and his ears were turning bright red.

"Jeremy? Please tell me. How long?"

When he spoke, his voice was so faint she could just barely hear him. "Um . . . about seventeen months."

"What?" She sat bolt upright so fast that her nose almost collided with his collarbone.

"Since the first week I met you, Pip." He spoke firmly and steadily, meeting her incredulous gaze unwaveringly, with eyes that held a plea for her understanding.

The thought of Jeremy loving her for all those months did funny things to her pulse rate. If only she'd known!

Then she remembered. "But that's impossible! What about Mary? You aren't claiming to have loved both of us at the same time, I hope?"

He had the grace to look embarrassed. "I'm afraid Mary doesn't exist. There's no such person. You see, I—"

Blue sky, green foliage, and Jeremy's face suddenly seemed to whirl before Pippi's eyes. "But I talked to her on the phone!"

"That was Larry's secretary. She thought she was helping me pull a practical joke on someone."

"Some joke!" She was so hurt and outraged she could scarcely speak. "How could you do such a thing to your worst enemy, let alone someone you claim to love? Did it give you a good laugh, driving me to the brink of insanity over a woman who doesn't even exist?"

"It was never a joke. Don't you understand, I thought it was the only way I could ever get you to see me as a man. I was just following *your* advice, Pip. Except that it was *you* I was courting!"

She stared at him, dazed and speechless, scarcely comprehending the incredible thing he was trying to tell her.

He gripped her by the shoulders as if by touch alone he could transmit the truth to the very heart of her being.

"Everything we planned, everything we rehearsed together I did in hopes of making you want me as much as I want you," he said. "I asked for your advice so you could teach me how you wanted to be loved."

"Oh, Jeremy." She was so moved by his words that for a long moment that was all she could say. He had courted her as no other woman had ever been courted. And yet, wouldn't it have saved them both so much pain and doubt if only . . .

"Why didn't you just tell me?" she asked softly.

"I tried, Pip. Lord knows I tried! It wasn't easy to speak out, but one day I finally felt both desperate enough and brave enough to risk it. I said the words. But you misunderstood me. You leaped to the crazy conclusion that I was talking about some other woman. Or even, as I recall, a man!"

"Omigosh! *That* day!" She blushed in mortification.

"Yes. That day. And then you proceeded to warn me that I'd be making a terrible mistake if I breathed one word of my feelings to the woman I loved!" He flashed her a rueful smile and let his fingers slide from her shoulders up to her neck as he bestowed a playful kiss on the tip of her nose. "Now do you understand why I didn't tell you?"

"Oh, Jeremy, I could just die!" she wailed,

burying her face against the solid warmth of his chest. "How can you love me when I'm the biggest fool that ever lived?"

"Loving you is easy, Pip. The hard part was being just your friend and nothing more." He stroked the curls at the nape of her neck and added thoughtfully, "I didn't like deceiving you, Pip. So many times it was on the tip of my tongue to confess the truth. But something always happened to hold it back. Like this morning."

"This morning?" she asked uneasily. Suddenly, the things he'd started to say at breakfast came back to her in a whole new light. She groaned and fell back flat against the roof. "I did it again, didn't I? Jumped to conclusions and made an ass out of myself!"

He leaned down and planted a quick kiss on her lips. "I'm curious. Exactly what conclusions did you jump to?"

"I thought you were politely giving me the brush-off and telling me that last night didn't mean a thing."

He shook his head in disbelief. "So you ended up making it sound as if it hadn't meant a thing to *you*! Just when I was within one breath of telling you I loved you!"

"Sorry." She gulped. "Bad timing, huh?"

"Very. Not only did you freeze that particular announcement on my lips, you also prevented me from apologizing."

"For what?"

"For the things I said last night." His eyes were troubled. "In the past, you've fallen for the wrong kind of guy and those relationships never lasted, no matter how hard you tried. Last night, I let that worry me. I knew I couldn't bear to be just another 'mistake' to you, Pip."

"Loving you is no mistake!"

"That's what *I* decided too," he informed her with a grin. "Because I'm not like those other guys. I'm not going to let you down, not ever. And I'm not going to let you fall out of love with me. What we have together is going to last, because *both* of us care enough to *make* it last."

Somehow she managed to speak past the lump in her throat. "Oh, Jeremy, I love you so much." She reached up and traced his crooked, tender, sexy smile.

"Until you," she said, "I'd never fallen in love this way—gradually, day by day, layer by layer, deeper and deeper, to the point where love is an indivisible part of me. Until you I'd never fallen in love with a friend who shared talk, fun, laughter, comfort, and handkerchiefs with me."

"Pip, you're making me blush."

"I'm not done yet. Until you I'd never fallen in love with a man who could take me soaring like a bird. And I don't mean just in your glider!" That *really* made him blush. "So you see," she whispered, "this time *is* different. I've never loved like this before."

"You've never *been* loved like this before either!" he vowed.

"You're so right!" she said, chuckling at the unintended double meaning of his words. She ran her hands up his chest and lowered her voice to a throaty drawl. "I noticed last night that your 'loving' was pretty darn special!"

He turned a full shade redder. "I didn't mean—"

"I know. But *I* meant every word. So, don't you think it's time we got down off this roof and found a slightly less precarious and more private location for finishing this conversation?"

"Good idea. But first, there's just one thing . . ."

"Uh-oh. What is it this time?"

"I need your advice again. Concerning a proposal of marriage. How do you suggest I go about it?"

"As swiftly and simply and straightforwardly as possible!"

"I see. Should I go down on bended knee, do you think?"

"That's up to you. You could try something really original, like standing on your head."

"As my lady wishes."

"Jeremy, no! I was just kidding! You'll fall and break your— Omigosh!"

"Miss Smith, will you do me the honor—"

"Yes! Anything! Just please—"

Beaming a euphoric smile, Jeremy lowered his feet back down to the roof. "You've just made me the happiest man alive!"

Pippi laughed shakily. "Thank heavens you *are* still alive, you lunatic! Now, if you can figure out how to get us safely down off this roof, then I'll be the happiest *woman* alive!"

"I suggest we use the ladder."

She stuck her tongue out at him. "Thanks a lot! Must you always take me so literally?"

She should have been warned by the warm, wicked sparkle in his eyes. "I'll take you any way I can get you, Pip." Without another word he picked her up, holding the length of her body tightly against his, and carried her down the ladder.

"O-mi-gosh," she sighed as he sprinted across the lawn toward the front door of his house. She had a remarkably silly grin on her face, but then, what could you expect from the happiest woman alive?

THE EDITOR'S CORNER

With this month's books we begin our *third* year of publishing LOVESWEPT. And are we excited about it! It feels as though we've only just begun, and I hope our enthusiasm for the love stories coming up next year is matched by your enjoyment of them.

Publishers work far in advance of the dates books reach the public. Did you know that producing a LOVESWEPT romance takes the same amount of time as a baby? That's right, nine full months! Even as you are reading this we are sending to our Production Department the LOVESWEPTS for January *1986*. So, with great certainty, I can assure you that our third year will continue the tradition of emotional and exceptional romances you've come to expect from LOVESWEPT. I envy you. I wish I had all the great forthcoming LOVESWEPTS to enjoy for the first time. But, then, you should just see what delicious stuff is on my desk right now for 1986! Back to next month, now, and the "four pleasures" in store for you.

Marvelous Barbara Boswell is back with **DARLING OBSTACLES,** LOVESWEPT #95. The title refers to the seven children the heroine and hero (both widowed) have between them. Never have there been seven more rowdy or adorable snags to romance. Maggie May is poor and very proud and the babysitter of surgeon Greg Wilder's three youngest children. Wrapped in their own concerns, neither parent has taken a good long look at the other until one chilly night when Greg comes to pick up his kids . . . and then the magic starts! **DARLING OBSTACLES** is genuinely heartwarming and deeply thrilling. Nine cheers for Barbara Boswell!

(continued)

Passionate and intense, **ENCHANTMENT,** LOVE-SWEPT #96, by Kimberli Wagner is a riveting love story full of sensual tension between two dramatic characters. Alex Kouris and Rhea Morgan are both artists and both mesmerized by one another when they meet. They know immediately that they are kindred souls . . . yet each has a problem to come to terms with before they can realize their destiny together. You won't want to miss Kim's breathtaking romance, which is truly full of **ENCHANTMENT.**

All of us on the LOVESWEPT staff are as fond of Adrienne Staff and Sally Goldenbaum as we are admiring of their skill at creating a unique love story. They make their debut with us in **WHAT'S A NICE GIRL . . . ?,** LOVESWEPT #97. This is the wonderfully humorous and truly touching romance of Susan Rosten and Logan Reed—two people who were meant to find one another across an ocean of differences. Susan comes from a boisterous, warm, close-knit Jewish family; Logan is a rather staid member of the "country club set." Susan owns and operates a local tavern; Logan is a distinguished physician. The resolution of the conflicts between them is often merry, sometimes serious, and always emotionally moving. We believe that after reading **WHAT'S A NICE GIRL . . . ?** you'll be as enthusiastic fans of Adrienne's and Sally's as we are.

And rounding out the month is a superb romance from that superb writer Fayrene Preston. **MISSISSIPPI BLUES,** LOVESWEPT #98, is as witty, as sensually evocative, as emotionally involving as a love story can be! You'll be delighted from the first moments of the provocative (and most unusual) opening of this story until the very last. Fayrene's brash Yankee hero, Kane Benedict, falls for winsome heroine, Suzanna de Francesca, a tenderhearted, passionate woman who has three extraordinary people for whom she's responsible. Suzanna's need to protect her home and its residents clashes violently with Kane's interest in her community. Yet the sultry attraction between them won't—*can't*—be stopped. The charm of Magnolia Trails and the love of Kane and Suzanna will linger with you long after you've finished **MISSISSIPPI BLUES.**

Enjoy!
Sincerely,

Carolyn Nichols

Carolyn Nichols
    Editor
LOVESWEPT
Bantam Books, Inc.
666 Fifth Avenue
New York, NY 10103

Dear Reader:

Meet Belinda Stuart—talented, beautiful, and about to embark on a new life as a successful painter. The only dark place in her heart is occupied by Jack, the tormented husband from whom she has had to separate. Suddenly, just as she's getting her act together, the past comes back to tear her apart.

Back in their carefree days at Harvard, Belinda and her best friend Sally met the men they would marry. Both Jack Stuart and Harry Granger were part of a group who jokingly referred to themselves as "the Ruffians," an irresistibly boisterous club whose loyalty to each other lasted long after their college years. Belinda, captivated by Jack's winning good looks and his talent as a writer, chose him over Harry, but it was Harry who went on to literary fame.

When Harry's hit musical opens in New York, all the Ruffians are there to cheer their friend's success. Two days later tragedy has struck—one of the Ruffians has been murdered, shot point blank in the doorway of Sally and Harry's house. And Belinda is forced to face the fact that the murder is related to her—although she has no idea why.

One by one, every man Belinda has known turns up in the present—Peter Venables, who once loved Belinda and can't believe she doesn't feel the same way for him; Mike Pierce, the perfect gentleman who treats Belinda like a beautiful younger sister; even Harry, Belinda and Jack's most trusted friend—each man with a conflicting story to tell. One is a cold-blooded killer; all prefer to blame Jack than face the horrible truth.

When Belinda and Jack were married, Sally was determined to give them the perfect wedding present, an antique wheel of fortune that would foretell their happy lives together. But now Belinda must return, alone, to the past. She has to uncover the dark secret that has already claimed the life of one person—and may soon claim her own.

Let Dana Clarins thrill you with Belinda's spellbinding story, the unforgettable tale of what happens when a beautiful woman wakes to find herself, alone and frightened, in the middle of her own worst nightmare.

Dana Clarins is a bestselling writer whose books have sold millions of copies under another name. GUILTY PARTIES is the best yet. I'm betting you won't be able to put it down!

Warm regards,

Nessa Rapoport

Nessa Rapoport
Senior Editor

S ALLY CAME OFF THE ELEVATOR carrying in her arms, like a gigantic infant, a cascade of yellow roses wrapped in tissue, tied loosely with a thick yellow ribbon, a floppy bow. She marched on into the kitchen and began searching for vases.

"What in the world—" I said.

"You've got paint all over your face, dear. Two vases aren't going to be enough." She was wearing a pale blue linen dress, sleeveless, with white piping. She was too pale herself for the outfit but with the jet-black hair and the sharp angles of her face she looked great.

I found her a third vase. "What is this?"

"For you. They were propped on that pathetic little wooden chair down in the lobby. Just sitting there. I asked a man carrying a box bigger than East Rutherford into the warehouse if he'd seen them delivered. He told me he couldn't see where he was going, let alone check out deliverymen. Here's a card."

I tore open the envelope.

Apologies are in order. I'll make them in person.

The fan on the counter passed its waves across my face like the flutter of invisible wings, and I felt a shiver ripple along my spine. Sally was watching me, hands on hips, feet apart, waiting impatiently. "So what does it say?"

I handed it to her and she cocked her head inquisitively. The light at the windows was reflecting the deep purple of the afternoon sky. The first raindrops were tapping on the skylight. I couldn't tell her about Venables. I'd told him I wouldn't and he was their houseguest on top of that and the show was opening and who needed any more problems?

And Sal and I didn't tell each other everything, anyway. Not anymore.

"May I ask what that is supposed to mean?"

I made a face. "It's nothing. A guy . . . a guy I barely know made a mistake the other night . . ." I shrugged.

"Ah, the adventures of the newly single!" She picked up two of the vases and smiled at me quizzically. "Well,

I won't pry. But let it be recorded that I am utterly fascinated."

"It's not very fascinating. Let that be recorded."

I followed her into the work area. The thunder's first crack went off like a cannon and I flinched. Like a child frightened by loud noises and the gathering darkness.

"I'm betting on Jack. Or—hmmm—could it be Mike?"

"What? What are you talking about?"

"Belinda, are you all right?"

"Yes, of course, I'm fine."

"The flowers. I was talking about the flowers—I'll bet they're from Jack, who misbehaved and is sorry . . . or from Mike. I mean, you have been seeing Mike—"

"Please, Sal. Mike is an old friend. You know that— we've had dinner a couple of times and Mike is the spitting image of Bertie Wooster and he's a dear. But he never, never would make a mistake about me. Okay? I rest my case."

Sally was leaning against the wheel-of-fortune, staring out into the rain, nodding. I mopped sweat from my face and dropped the towel on the table.

"All right, all right. It's your secret." She pressed a forefinger to her lips, looking at me from the corners of her eyes. . . .

The afternoon wore on. The loft darkened. Lightning continued to crackle over the city like electrical stems, jagged, plunging down into the heart of Manhattan. The rain came down like dishwater emptying out of a sink. Sally had another drink and sucked on the bright green wedge of lime. The yellow roses glowed as if they were lit from within. I listened to Sally talk about men, the show, Harry and Jack. . . .

One moment she was laughing and then the thunder hammered at the skylight again and her face began to come apart and redefine itself as if she were about to burst into tears.

"Are you all right, Sal?" I went to her, wanting to help. She turned quickly away, back to the wheel-of-fortune.

"Let's see what the gods hold for tonight, a hit or a miss." She sniffled, spun the wheel, planted her feet apart as if challenging the future. It finally clicked to a halt.

Sal read it slowly. "'You will have everything you have hoped for.'"

She looked at me, trying to smile.

"Oh," she said, "everything is such a mess, honey." She began to cry with her head on my shoulder. I put my arm around her, felt the shuddering as Sally clung to me. I cooed to her. Everything would be all right. But as I stroked her shiny black hair, the paintings in the shadows caught my eye and I wasn't sure.

* * *

AT SIX O'CLOCK THE CROWD clogged the street in front of the theater, the lucky ones squeezed beneath the marquee with its *Scoundrels All!* logo in Harvard crimson. Everyone was dressed up and soaked through with perspiration and sprays of rain. Everyone seemed to be shouting to be heard, faces were red, laughter too loud. Bright, artificial smiles looked like the direct result of root-canal work. Hope was everywhere. The sight made me wonder if my own opening would be so frantic, so harried, so riddled with fear and tension.

I held onto Mike's arm, smiled faintly at familiar faces, and nodded at snatches of conversation I couldn't quite make out. The whole scene was a kind of orgy of self-consciousness, people with a good deal to lose but trying not to show it, pretending that nothing hung in the balance. Another opening, another show.

Harry's head was visible above the crowd, inclined to the comments of two men I recognized by sight, one a legendary womanizer and show-business angel, the other a famous agent who knew everyone and never missed anything. At a party once years before I'd seen him take a package of chewing gum from the beringed hand of a very young woman with turquoise and purple hair and Jack had whispered to me: "See that? That's how they do it. Cocaine wrapped in five little sticks, like gum." He'd been terribly amused when at first I couldn't believe it.

A large, bulky man in a very crumpled linen jacket with a floppy silk handkerchief dribbling from the pocket looked benignly out across the crowd from Harry's side. He alone seemed serene and somewhat amused by the proceedings, as if his cumbersome size kept him from becoming too frantic. I'd seen him before, I was sure of it, but where? I was watching him without really being aware of it when he caught my eye, seemed to be staring at me, expressionless. Then, as if he'd made a connection that was just eluding me, he slowly grinned and I looked away. Should I have known him? He wasn't the type you'd forget.

Mike was waving at people, chattering away. The show's director stood more or less alone, a tiny bearded man, looking like a child's toy wound right to the breaking point. He glanced at his watch, then disappeared through the stage door. Slowly the crowd began to push through the doors, through the lobby, down the red-carpeted aisles toward their seats. The black uniformed ushers whisked up and down, checking tickets, handing out programs.

My stomach was knotted, my throat dry, and I wondered how Sally was holding up. I couldn't see her in the crowd. Mike Nichols was a few rows ahead of us, standing, still wearing a rain-spotted, belted trench coat, his face amazingly boyish beneath the blondish hair. There was Tony LoBianco, dark and handsome, radiating energy and intensity, as if he were about to spring at someone or something. Doc Simon, shy and tall and scholarly, was talking to a man who looked like a banker, which figured, since the playwright had finally, officially, made all the money in the known universe.

Scanning the faces, I knew I was actually looking for the two I hoped most weren't there. Jack. And Peter Venables. The thought of both men was pushing my stomach off center. Praying I wouldn't turn and come face to face with them, praying for the easy way out. I kept thinking of Jack slamming the phone down and cutting Sally off . . . and Peter's beautiful yellow roses and the note that filled me with dread. *Apologies are in order. I'll make them in person.*

Finally, thank God, the houselights dimmed and I hadn't seen either of them.

Within seconds I felt as if the curtain had gone up on a kind of personal psychodrama, as if I'd stumbled straight off the edge of the real world and was free-falling through time.

★   ★   ★

FOR SOME REASON THAT SUMMER nobody had quite bothered to prepare me for the show I saw. Maybe it was because I had been so wrapped up in my own work, maybe because I hadn't been listening when they tried. Whatever the reason, I wasn't in the least prepared once the actors and actresses had taken the stage, and it was hard to shake free of the disorientation.

With music and dancing and a witty book, *Scoundrels All!* was *our* story, the story of the Ruffians and Sally and me, and it came at me in a series of waves, reviving memories I'd never known were buried in my subconscious, memories of people and events I hadn't been aware of at the time. It was like seeing one of Alex Katz's paintings in a Fifty-seventh Street gallery, a scene of his sharp-featured people at a cocktail party, pretty women with flat, predatory looks, well-dressed men with cuffs showing just the right amount as they climbed one social or business ladder after another . . . like seeing the paintings and slowly realizing that you were there, you'd been one of the people at the party. It was both unnerving and seductive and I felt myself almost guiltily being excited by what I saw, as if it were my own private secret.

I'd been so wrapped up in my own concerns in those days that I'd hardly noticed the world around me. Classes, clothes, time spent with Sally, driving her little red convertible along narrow leaf-blown roads, working in the studio at all hours, painting and losing track of time, then meeting Harry Granger . . . and later Jack Stuart.

Now, astonished, I watched all our lives cavorting across the stage, laughter rippling and applause exploding from the audience. Reality had been softened and given pastel hues at it was filtered through the lens of nostalgia. Like a faint recollection that had almost slipped through the cracks of memory, my past was coming back to life, and we were all up there on the stage. Whatever names they were called, they were us. Jack, the athlete with the handsome face, tossing a football in the air, singing a song about the big game Saturday with Yale . . . Mike wearing white duck slacks and a straw boater at a jaunty angle, dancing an engaging soft-shoe . . . Harry politicking his friends about his idea for a club, an oath of loyalty, and a commitment for a lifetime, all so innocent and idealistic . . . and there were the girls, a blond and a brunette arriving on the stage in a snazzy red convertible.

I was having some difficulty keeping the lines between fact and fiction from blurring. Which was the real Belinda? The one on stage or the nearly middle-aged one watching? Did I really say that? Is that the way I behaved, the way I appeared to others—the self-centered ultra-Wasp who seemed to pluck for herself first one man and then the other?

The love stories wound sinuously, sometimes comically, through the saga of the founding of the club and the conflicts among the members and the crisis of the football game . . . Harry falling in love with the blond, then losing her to Jack, then Harry taking sudden notice of the brunette.

But it was all in a kind of fairyland where the hurts never lasted and everybody finally loved everyone else and everything was all right. . . . Jack was singing alone in a spotlight, wearing a corny letter sweater with the flickering illusion of a pep-rally bonfire through a scrim behind him. Not much like Harvard, really, it might have been an artifact like the Thurber and Nugent play, *The Male Animal*, it all seemed so quaint and long ago. Jack was singing about the blond girl he'd fallen for and how he was going to have to take her away from his best pal Harry and would it wreck their friendship and how could one Scoundrel do such a thing to another?

And, like a sentimental fool, I thanked God for the darkness of the theater. My cheek was wet with tears.

A stunning novel of romance and intrigue by

THE FOREVER DREAM

by Iris Johansen

Tania Orlinov is prima ballerina for a New York ballet company. Jared Ryker is a brilliant scientist whose genetics research has brought him to the brink of discovering how to extend human life for up to 500 years. A chance meeting brings them together—and now nothing can keep them apart.

THE FOREVER DREAM has all the passion, extraordinarily sensual lovemaking and romance that have become Iris Johansen's signature, plus the tension and suspense of a first-rate thriller. In her longest and most far-reaching novel to date, Iris Johansen taps all our fantasies of romantic love and explores the fascinating implications of practical immortality.

Don't miss THE FOREVER DREAM, available wherever Bantam Books are sold, or use this handy coupon for ordering:

#1 HEAVEN'S PRICE
By Sandra Brown
Blair Simpson had enclosed herself in the fortress of her dancing, but Sean Garrett was determined to love her anyway. In his arms she came to understand the emotions behind her dancing. But could she afford the high price of love?

#2 SURRENDER
By Helen Mittermeyer
Derry had been pirated from the church by her ex-husband, from under the nose of the man she was to marry. She remembered every detail that had driven them apart—and the passion that had drawn her to him. The unresolved problems between them grew . . . but their desire swept them toward surrender.

#3 THE JOINING STONE
By Noelle Berry McCue
Anger and desire warred within her, but Tara Burns was determined not to let Damon Mallory know her feelings. When he'd walked out of their marriage, she'd been hurt.

Damon had violated a sacred trust, yet her passion for him was as breathtaking as the Grand Canyon.

#4 SILVER MIRACLES
By Fayrene Preston
Silver-haired Chase Colfax stood in the Texas moonlight, then took Trinity Ann Warrenton into his arms. Overcome by her own needs, yet determined to have him on her own terms, she struggled to keep from losing herself in his passion.

#5 MATCHING WITS
By Carla Neggers
From the moment they met, Ryan Davis tried to outmaneuver Abigail Lawrence. She'd met her match in the Back Bay businessman. And Ryan knew the Boston lawyer was more woman than any he'd ever encountered. Only if they vanquished their need to best the other could their love triumph.

#6 A LOVE FOR ALL TIME
By Dorothy Garlock
A car crash had left its marks on Casey Farrow's beauty. So what were Dan

Murdock's motives for pursuing her? Guilt? Pity? Casey had to choose. She could live with doubt and fear . . . or learn a lesson in love.

#7 A TRYST WITH MR. LINCOLN?
By Billie Green
When Jiggs O'Malley awakened in a strange hotel room, all she saw were the laughing eyes of stranger Matt Brady . . . all she heard were his teasing taunts about their "night together" . . . and all she remembered was nothing! They evaded the passions that intoxicated them until . . . there was nowhere to flee but into each other's arms.

#8 TEMPTATION'S STING
By Helen Conrad
Taylor Winfield likened Rachel Davidson to a Conus shell, contradictory and impenetrable. Rachel battled for independence, torn by her need for Taylor's embraces and her impassioned desire to be her own woman. Could they both succumb to the temptation of the tropical paradise and still be true to their hearts?

#9 DECEMBER 32nd . . . AND ALWAYS
By Marie Michael
Blaise Hamilton made her feel like the most desirable woman on earth. Pat opened herself to emotions she'd thought buried with her late husband. Together they were unbeatable as they worked to build the jet of her late husband's dreams. Time seemed to be running out and yet—would ALWAYS be long enough?

#10 HARD DRIVIN' MAN
By Nancy Carlson
Sabrina sensed Jacy in hot pursuit, as she maneuvered her truck around the racetrack, and recalled his arms clasping her to him. Was he only using her feelings so he could take over her trucking company? Their passion knew no limits as they raced full speed toward love.

#11 BELOVED INTRUDER
By Noelle Berry McCue
Shannon Douglas hated

Michael Brady from the moment he brought the breezes of life into her shadowy existence. Yet a specter of the past remained to torment her and threaten their future. Could he subdue the demons that haunted her, and carry her to true happiness?

#12 HUNTER'S PAYNE
By Joan J. Domning
P. Lee Payne strode into Karen Hunter's office demanding to know why she was stalking him. She was determined to interview the mysterious photographer. She uncovered his concealed emotions, but could the secrets their hearts confided protect their love, or would harsh daylight shatter their fragile alliance?

#13 TIGER LADY
By Joan J. Domning
Who *was* this mysterious lover she'd never seen who courted her on the office computer, and nicknamed her Tiger Lady? And could he compete with Larry Hart, who came to repair the computer and stayed to short-cir-

cuit her emotions? How could she choose between poetry and passion—between soul and Hart?

#14 STORMY VOWS
By Iris Johansen
Independent Brenna Sloan wasn't strong enough to reach out for the love she needed, and Michael Donovan knew only how to take—until he met Brenna. Only after a misunderstanding nearly destroyed their happiness, did they surrender to their fiery passion.

#15 BRIEF DELIGHT
By Helen Mittermeyer
Darius Chadwick felt his chest tighten with desire as Cygnet Melton glided into his life. But a prelude was all they knew before Cyg fled in despair, certain she had shattered the dream they had made together. Their hearts had collided in an instant; now could they seize the joy of enduring love?

#16 A VERY RELUCTANT KNIGHT
By Billie Green
A tornado brought them together in a storm cel-

She said brightly, 'What would you like to talk about?' This was terrible, the worst evening of her whole life.

'The boat,' he suggested tightly, getting the car out into the traffic without hitting anyone, although someone was angrily blaring away on a horn. 'I left it there. I told you. I put it in bond, and it's there at the marina. It can stay there for as long as I pay the moorage and the bond charge every six months.' He shrugged, and said harshly, 'All right. Yes. I'd like to move into your house.'

She heard the noise she made, a cross between a gasp and a squeak. 'Why do you——? I—all right.' She tried to tell her heart to slow down, be calm. There would be time. He wasn't running away. He didn't hate her, and maybe there would be a day when he could love her. 'There's the second bedroom,' she offered, 'and a kind of study I don't use. I was cleaning it out today. Actually, it—you could have it.' She could breathe, she found, and maybe she could even talk. She knew he had not meant that he wanted her, his voice had told her that. In the world he'd been living in, taking on crew was a casual thing, and didn't seem to mean the same thing as living with someone. Maybe he thought her rash offer to share the house was a business deal. He must think that. Oh, lord! Was he expecting to pay rent? She said steadily, 'When do you want to move in?'

He didn't answer. Was he having second thoughts? No wonder. She was behaving like a nutcase, and who wanted a crazy for a landlady? She said, 'I'm not much of a cook. Cathy's worse, I'm afraid, and she's the one cooking the dinners because that's the deal I made and she'd take off if she wasn't earning her way. She lives in the downstairs apartment and—well, you know that, don't you? Anyway, Barry sometimes cooks and she—I'm sorry, but the menu's not going to be as——'

He jerked the car around and she found herself hanging on to the dashboard, staring at the car park for Kits beach. She swallowed and said dully, 'It's not going to work, is it? I'm sorry.'

'It's going to work.' He was breathing oddly, not looking at her. He shoved the lever into park. Then, after a second, he turned the lights off, then the engine. 'Let's go for a walk. I need the air.'

It was dark. She walked at his side, slipping awkwardly in the sand and finally taking off her heels and walking in her stockings through the sand. He was staring out at the boats anchored in English bay, their lights reflecting in the water.

'You're going to miss the boat, aren't you?' She caught her hand reaching for his, jerked it back and stood a little farther away. 'Are you going to bring it back here?'

What would he say if she told him she loved him? He knew, didn't he? But——

'Not yet.' He turned and stared down at her. Now she didn't have heels on he seemed a lot taller, although she was a tall girl. 'Holidays, I thought.' His jaw worked and he said grimly, 'I thought maybe—well, maybe you'd like to come down and spend holidays on the boat. With me.'

She touched her lips with her tongue. They dried again instantly. 'But why?' She sucked in a lungful of air. 'I—it doesn't matter why. I——'

'Because I need you.' His voice was harsh, and

she forgot to breathe. 'Because ever since you walked into my life I've been discovering that when you were there—when—there were colours and sounds and . . . and life.' His arms reached, took her shoulders very gently between his hands. 'Dinah, I know you're—you need time. But . . .' His voice dropped to a whisper and he said, '*Señorita*, you make me want all the things I thought I would never have again. Loving. You.'

She saw him gulp and she tried to speak, but her throat was seized, frozen. He said, 'Dinah, you scare the hell out of me. You were just there, on that mountain in the Baja, and my heart wanted to stop beating for the beauty of the world. It was as if I'd been in a shadow all my life, and you turned the world into light and colour.'

'Why did you come back?' she asked on a whisper. She found that she dared to lift her hands, to explore the hardness of his chest through his suit jacket.

'Because you're here. Because it was time.' His fingers tightened and he said, 'I want to share your home, Dinah. I want to see you frowning over a painting that's not going right, the smile in your eyes when it works. I want to share your worries over those girls.' She saw him swallow. 'I want more. When you're ready to trust me with your life, I want you . . . in my bed and my heart and—I love you, Dinah.'

'Oh,' she breathed.

His fingers straightened, then curled into her upper arms. 'I—I think you could love me, too. You said it once, and I know you've regretted saying that, but I think if you let yourself you'd——'

'I didn't regret it. I thought you didn't want to hear it.' She could feel his gasp, his heart thundering through the jacket. She moved her hands and slipped them under the jacket, felt his heat through the crisp cotton shirt. She whispered, 'Would you like to hear it?'

He nodded. She felt his arms drawing her close and her voice strengthened. 'I love you. I love you, Joe Mitchell. I asked you to live in my house because I want you in my life. I want your babies.' She hesitated, but his lips were descending on to hers.

'Enough talking,' he growled, as he drew her soft eagerness against his hard male body. 'Enough. It's time for loving.' His lips took hers, his tongue exploring her eager mouth. 'Oh, *señorita*, I've been so hungry for you.'

When she could, she laughed, a husky, joyful sound. 'I love it when you call me *señorita*, Joe. I love you. It reminds me of when you kissed me up there on that mountain. I—I wanted you so much.'

He laughed, then his lips covered hers again, loving and demanding. 'We'll have to find another pet name,' he growled. 'You're not going to be a *señorita* for long. How about *mi esposa*—my wife?' He took her gasp with his lips, his mouth, murmured, 'I think one unwed mother in that house of yours is quite enough.' Then his laughter died and he said raggedly, 'You are going to marry me, aren't you?'

'Yes, darling. Yes.' Then, for a long time, she couldn't say anything else.

Take 4 bestselling love stories FREE

Plus get a FREE surprise gift!

In December,
let Harlequin warm your heart with the
AWARD OF EXCELLENCE title

Harlequin Presents...

PENNY JORDAN

a rekindled passion

Over twenty years ago, Kate had a holiday
affair with Joss Bennett and found herself
pregnant as a result. Believing that Joss had
abandoned her to return to his wife and child,
Kate had her daughter and made no attempt
to track Joss down.

At her daughter's wedding, Kate suddenly
confronts the past in the shape of the
bridegroom's distant relative—Joss. He quickly
realises that Sophy must be his daughter and
wonders why Kate never contacted him.

Can love be rekindled after twenty years?
Be sure not to miss this AWARD OF EXCELLENCE
title, available wherever Harlequin books
are sold.

HP-KIND-1

Harlequin Superromance

THEY'RE A BREED APART

The men and women of the Canadian prairies are slow to give their friendship or their love. On the prairies, such gifts can never be recalled. Friendships between families last for generations. And love, once lit, burns hot and pure and bright for a lifetime.

In honor of this special breed of men and women, Harlequin Superromance® presents:

SAGEBRUSH AND SUNSHINE
(Available in October)

and

MAGIC AND MOONBEAMS
(Available in December)

two books by Margot Dalton, featuring the Lyndons and the Burmans, prairie families joined for generations by friendship, then nearly torn apart by love.

Look for SUNSHINE in October and MOONBEAMS in December, coming to you from Harlequin.

MAG-C1R

Harlequin romances are now available in stores at these convenient times each month.

Harlequin Presents
Harlequin American Romance
Harlequin Historical
Harlequin Intrigue

These series will be in stores on the 4th of every month.

Harlequin Romance
Harlequin Temptation
Harlequin Superromance
Harlequin Regency Romance

New titles for these series will be in stores on the 16th of every month.

We hope this new schedule is convenient for you. With only two trips each month to your local bookseller, you will always be sure not to miss any of your favorite authors!

Happy reading!

Please note there may be slight variations in on-sale dates in your area due to differences in shipping and handling.

lar. But Maggie Sims and Mark Wilding were anything but perfectly matched. Maggie wanted to prove he was wrong about her. She knew they didn't belong together, but when he caressed her, she was swept up in a passion that promised a lifetime of love.

#17 TEMPEST AT SEA
By Iris Johansen
Jane Smith sneaked aboard playboy-director Jake Dominic's yacht on a dare. The muscled arms that captured her were inescapable—and suddenly Jane found herself agreeing to a month-long cruise of the Caribbean. Jane had never given much thought to love, but under Jake's tutelage she discovered its magic . . . and its torment.

#18 AUTUMN FLAMES
By Sara Orwig
Lily Dunbar had ventured too far into the wilderness of Reece Wakefield's vast Chilean ranch; now an oncoming storm thrust her into his arms . . . and he refused to let her go. Could he lure her, step by seductive step, away from the life she had forged for herself, to find her real home in his arms?

#19 PFARR LAKE AFFAIR
By Joan J. Domning
Leslie Pfarr hadn't been back at her father's resort for an hour before she was pitched into the lake by Eric Nordstrom! The brash teenager who'd made her childhood a constant torment had grown into a handsome man. But when he began persuading her to fall in love, Leslie wondered if she was courting disaster.

#20 HEART ON A STRING
By Carla Neggers
One look at heart surgeon Paul Houghton Welling told JoAnna Radcliff he belonged in the stuffy society world she'd escaped for a cottage in Pigeon Cove. She firmly believed she'd never fit into his life, but he set out to show her she was wrong. She was the puppet master, but he knew how to keep her heart on a string.

#21 THE SEDUCTION OF JASON
By Fayrene Preston
On vacation in Martinique, Morgan Saunders found Jason Falco. When a misunderstanding drove him away, she had to win him back. She played the seductress to tempt him to return; she sent him tropical flowers to tantalize him; she wrote her love in letters twenty feet high—on a billboard that echoed the words in her heart.

#22 BREAKFAST IN BED
By Sandra Brown
For all Sloan Fairchild knew, Hollywood had moved to San Francisco when mystery writer Carter Madison stepped into her bed-and-breakfast inn. In his arms the forbidden longing that throbbed between them erupted. Sloan had to choose—between her love for him and her loyalty to a friend . . .

#23 TAKING SAVANNAH
By Becky Combs
The Mercedes was headed straight for her! Cassie hurled a rock that smashed the antique car's taillight. The price driver Jake Kilrain exacted was a passionate kiss, and he set out to woo the Southern lady, Cassie, but discovered that his efforts to conquer the lady might end in his own surrender . . .

#24 THE RELUCTANT LARK
By Iris Johansen
Her haunting voice had earned Sheena Reardon fame as Ireland's mournful dove. Yet to Rand Challon the young singer was not just a lark but a woman whom he desired with all his heart. Rand knew he could teach her to spread her wings and fly free, but would her flight take her from him or into his arms forever?